MURDER
IN THE AIR

A high-flyer comes crashing down in
this thrilling Irish murder mystery

DAVID PEARSON

THE
BOOK
FOLKS

Paperback edition published by

The Book Folks

London, 2018

© David Pearson

ISBN 978-1-7918-7373-8

www.thebookfolks.com

For Bessy, for all her help and support over the years.

Chapter One

Gerald Fortune, known by all and sundry as just 'Ger', stood in the small portacabin that served as a briefing room and terminal for the airport on Inis Mór, the largest of the Aran Islands off the coast of Galway. He was on the phone to Galway Airport, filing a flight plan for the journey back to the mainland.

"Take off from Inis Mór at eleven hundred hours, then a right turn out to Inverin not above 1500 feet, then on to Moycullen and Claregalway, expect a right-hand turn for Galway runway two-six at Claregalway. Call you at Moycullen, roger."

"And can you just confirm the number of souls on board please?" the controller at Galway said.

"Three souls on board: my architect, Fionn Devaney, my daughter Emma Fortune, and myself."

"Thanks, Mr Fortune. Once you are overhead Inverin, squawk 4420 on your transponder for radar identification. Have a good flight," the controller said, signing off.

Ger noted the number down on the notepad that would be strapped to his knee during the flight, along with a map of the route to be followed.

He walked the short distance out to the Cessna 172 that stood on the apron of Inis Mór airport. The two passengers were already on board, and Ger called to them as he approached the plane.

"Just doing the final walk around to check that everything is in order. I'll be with you in a minute. We have to take off at eleven," he said, looking at his watch. It was 10:55. He walked slowly around the little blue and white plane, examining the tyres, the flaps, rudder and lights to see that everything was moving freely and in good condition, before climbing into the left-hand seat and closing the door.

Ger was one of the fifty-eight members of the Atlantic Flying Club based at Galway airport. The club owned three Cessna 172s, and any club member that was in possession of a valid private pilot's license could hire one of the planes on a first-come, first-served basis for an hourly fee. Ger had been largely instrumental in building the club up to its current strength, and had ploughed quite a bit of his own money into the venture, so he tended to get preference when it came to getting a plane.

The three of them had flown out the previous day, and had spent the afternoon surveying the site of what Ger hoped would become a thirty-bedroomed hotel, once detailed plans were submitted to Galway County Council.

Ger Fortune had made his money initially in the north-west of England. He left Galway as soon as he had finished school, and had gone to stay with an uncle and aunt in Manchester, where he quickly found work in the building trade that was enjoying a resurgence after being in the doldrums for most of the 1980s.

He had started out like many Irishmen before him, carrying bricks, but he was a quick learner and it wasn't long before he became a bricklayer and was earning more money than he ever thought possible at that trade. He was careful with his money too, avoiding the double pitfalls of gambling and excessive drink that had reduced many of his fellow countrymen to penury, and when he returned to Ireland in 2004, he quickly developed a nice little business building small strings of semi-detached houses which sold at substantial profit on the back of the now infamous Celtic Tiger.

By the time the recession came in 2008, Ger had amassed quite a large amount of money, but unlike many of his contemporaries, he sensed the arrival of the crash and got out of the business just in time.

With cash at hand, he was able to buy a number of sites at knock-down prices from bankrupt builders as the financial crisis deepened, so that when things began to improve again, he was ideally positioned to take best advantage.

These days, he no longer built houses himself. Instead, he partnered with builders: he provided the sites, and the builders actually constructed the properties. The proceeds of sale were split 60/40 between the builder and Ger himself under this arrangement. It was an ingenious system, leaving Ger free to pursue other opportunities while not having to worry about direct labour or sub-contractors or any of the hundreds of daily problems that plague the building trade, while all along making good money from his earlier astute investments.

Now equipped with a large war chest, Ger was keen to embark upon his next business venture – the construction of a very luxurious small hotel on Inis Mór. The hotel would be sold as part of a package to overseas clients. The package would include an air taxi ride from Galway to the island, using the services of the flying club, spa treatment and haute cuisine at the hotel, and various excursions around the beautiful west coast of Ireland both by plane and road vehicle, all at a fairly hefty price.

Needless to say, there was considerable resistance to Ger's plans from some of the locals on the island, though as was typical, opinion was divided. Some relished the additional employment that the venture would bring, while others detested the commercialization of the island believing the natural tranquillity and unspoilt beauty of the place would be destroyed forever.

Once seated inside the rather cramped cockpit of the little plane, Ger checked all the instruments to make sure everything was in order, and started the engine.

"Echo India X-ray Alpha Tango ready for taxi", he said into the radio.

"Roger, Alpha Tango, clear to line up runway three-two," the Inis Mór controller replied.

Ger released the parking brake, advanced the throttle and the plane moved gently forward. He lined it up on runway three-two as instructed, and moments later the controller called him again.

"Alpha Tango cleared take off runway three-two, right turn out to Inverin, wind two eighty at ten knots."

Ger blipped the radio again to signal that he had received the transmission.

"Emma, are you belted in?" Ger said.

"Yes, Dad, of course."

"Good. Here we go then."

He pushed the throttle to full power and the plane accelerated down the paved surface. As it gathered speed, Ger put in some rudder to keep it on the centre-line, and well before the end of the runway, he eased back on the yoke and the Cessna lifted cleanly into the air, crabbing slightly against the force of the stiff breeze.

When the plane was at a couple of hundred feet, and Ger had commenced the right turn to bring the aircraft on course for Inverin, just ten minutes away, the radio crackled into life again.

"Alpha Tango, off at eleven-oh-two. When ready, contact Galway on one-one-eight decimal seven. Good day."

"Thanks, Séan. Will do, one-one-eight decimal seven. Bye."

With the wind now largely behind them, the Cessna made Inverin in just over twelve minutes. Ger rotated the dial on the transponder to 4420, and called Galway. He was asked to press the 'ident' button on the transponder, and the Galway controller confirmed that he had been identified on their radar.

"Alpha Tango, continue as cleared not above fifteen hundred feet. Call us at Claregalway for the approach," the Galway controller said.

"Roger, call at Claregalway, Alpha Tango," Ger repeated.

The two passengers were enjoying the scenery in the bright summer sky. Cotton wool clouds drifted by overhead, and the dappled sunshine created a light and dark patchwork pattern on the boggy ground beneath them.

They were about half way between Inverin and Moycullen, flying along at fifteen hundred feet, being buffeted slightly by the breeze, when the engine stuttered to a halt.

"What's happening, Ger?" Fionn said with considerable alarm in his voice.

"Dad, dad," shrieked Emma from the back seat.

Ger checked all the instruments on the panel in front of him. The fuel gauge indicated there was plenty of fuel. The rev counter was at zero, and the plane began to pitch forward.

Ger attempted to start the engine again. Although the propeller rotated slowly under the input from the starter motor, the engine wouldn't catch, and the angle of descent became steeper.

Ger pulled back on the yoke to try and bring the nose up. He might be able to glide the plane down to earth if he couldn't get the engine going again.

He pressed the radio's transmit button.

"Mayday, Mayday. Alpha Tango has lost its engine, descending rapidly."

"Christ, do something Ger, for God's sake!" Fionn shouted, now completely panicked.

Emma was crying in the rear seat.

"Dad, dad. What's happening?" she sobbed.

"Start, ya bastard, start!" Ger shouted at the plane.

Ger Fortune tried again in vain to start the engine of the plane as the nose pitched forward again, despite the back pressure on the yoke. The airspeed was getting dangerously close to stall speed, and although the engine coughed as Ger operated the starter motor with the throttle advanced to the halfway point, it just wouldn't fire up.

"We're going in!" Ger shouted. "Brace, brace!"

The plane struck the bog nose first, and tumbled over sideways on its roof, ripping off the left-hand wing. Inside the cabin, Emma was thrown first against the side wall of the plane, and then her head was wrenched forward, striking the back of Fionn Devaney's seat with such force that it snapped her neck. The two men in the front didn't fare any better, and by the time the plane came to rest, all three occupants were dead.

A couple of lapwings that had been nesting in the bog took off, disturbed by the sudden drama. Then a terrible stillness descended on the scene, and aviation fuel seeped out onto the marshy ground.

Chapter Two

Senior Detective Inspector Maureen Lyons was at her desk in the office that had been allocated to her in the building close to Mill Street Garda Station in Galway. Things had changed considerably in recent months for the Galway Detective Unit. Lyons' partner, Mick Hays, had been made up to Detective Superintendent, and now spent a lot of his time on administrative duties, attending meetings and filling out endless reports. He didn't have a lot of interaction with the front-line officers, except that every two weeks there was a sort of team meeting which he attended if he was around, when progress on current cases – or lack of it – was discussed in detail.

Lyons had recently been joined by a new inspector – James Bolger. Bolger was an experiment. The Garda had been trying to modernise the force, and had looked to Europe for new ways of working. This had led them to allow entry at Inspector level to a few – very few – graduates of criminology, who had undergone a curtailed training programme in Garda procedure. The experiment was being carefully watched by senior management in the force, with a view to extending it if it was deemed to be successful.

Bolger had been careful to try and fit in. He had been parachuted into the Galway Detective Unit when Superintendent Plunkett had been given the go-ahead to expand the team. Bolger was inserted above Detective Sergeants Eamon Flynn and Sally Fahy, and under Maureen Lyons who now had Hays' old job title of Senior Inspector. Flynn and Fahy had been well prepared for Bolger's arrival, and had decided not to make any hasty decisions about the efficacy of the arrangement. A lot would depend on his attitude to them, though Flynn in particular couldn't help but be a little bit put out. He was inclined to refer to Bolger when he was out of earshot as 'the boy wonder'.

Lyons' phone rang.

"Lyons," she said.

"Hi, Inspector. We've had a call from Galway Mountain Rescue. It seems a plane has gone down somewhere out west. They've scrambled the helicopter, but they want someone from here to attend as well," the desk sergeant said.

"Oh, OK. Have we got a precise location?" she asked.

"They said to call the airport. They'll give you the low down," he said.

"Thanks, we'll call them now," she said, hanging up.

Lyons summoned her new recruit from the open-plan. She explained to Bolger what she had been told, and asked him to call the airport to get as much information as he could about the incident. He was back in her office three minutes later.

"It's a light aircraft with three people on board. It disappeared off the radar between Inverin and Moycullen. The helicopter is going out with a medical team, but it will be back at the airport in about half an hour, and they can give us a lift to the scene if you like," Bolger said.

"Sounds OK. I haven't been in a helicopter before. Are you up for it?"

"Sure. I'll get a radio so we can talk to the air sea rescue folks as we travel. Ready in five," Bolger said.

Lyons wasn't particularly fond of the slick way Bolger spoke, but he was from Dublin after all, so maybe everyone up there talks that way these days, she thought to herself.

* * *

They arrived at Galway airport just as the big red and white coastguard helicopter was landing, having delivered a small team of first responders out to the crash site. Lyons strolled over to where the captain of the chopper was alighting and introduced herself.

"Good morning, Captain, I'm DI Lyons from the Galway Detective Unit, and this is my colleague, DI Bolger," she said gesturing towards the effete figure of the younger man.

"Good morning, Inspector. My name is Brian O'Neill," the pilot said extending his hand.

"What's the scene like out at the crash?" Bolger asked, almost too quickly.

"Well it looks as if all three occupants have lost their lives, but that will need to be confirmed by the medics. The plane is a mess, and the site is virtually inaccessible except by helicopter, though you might just be able to get a good 4x4 to it if you were careful. There's an untarred road about a mile away to the south."

"Any idea why it crashed?" Lyons said.

"Not for me to say, Inspector. These light aircraft suffer a crazy failure rate, though in fairness, they are not always fatal, so the general public don't usually get to hear about them. But we encounter it all the time," O'Neill said.

"I see. The people here said you might be able to give us a lift out to the site, if that's OK?" Lyons said.

"Yes, that's fine. I'm just waiting for the Irish Aviation Authority Inspectors to get here. They're on their way from Dublin. They should be here in a few minutes. As soon as they get here, we'll get going. If you come into the office with us, we should be able to rustle up a cup of tea while we're waiting."

O'Neill, his co-pilot, and the two detectives made their way across to the coastguard building, which although rudimentary, seemed to have everything one would need for their particular kind of operation.

O'Neill's co-pilot, Jane Wells, busied herself making tea and retrieving a packet of biscuits from the cupboard over the sink, along with four mugs. She waited for the kettle to boil and then made a large pot of strong tea which she placed on the table, saying, "Tea's up. Help yourselves."

As they set about the refreshments, the radio O'Neill was wearing on the front of his jacket crackled to life.

"Romeo Juliet short finals for two-six," said the voice on the radio.

The Galway controller came back quickly, "Romeo Juliet clear to land runway two-six, wind two-eighty at twelve."

The small white twin-engined jet came into sight approaching the runway with its wheels dangling beneath it, flared as it crossed the threshold, landed with a small puff of smoke from the tyres, and came to a crawl on the runway with the aid of a loud, reverse thrust from the engines. The little jet, which had no marking of any kind on it other than the registration stencilled in black letters on the rear fuselage, taxied to the apron and shut down. The door opened, and a man and a woman dressed in business clothes descended onto the concrete and walked towards the coastguard building.

"Ah, Fergal, welcome to Galway," Brian O'Neill said as the two inspectors entered the building. "You're just in time for tea. Good flight down?"

"A bit bumpy on the approach, but yes, no issues. This is Sandra Jameson," the inspector said, introducing the second inspector to the small group.

When the introductions were complete, O'Neill turned to Lyons, "Fergal and I go way back. We trained together at Baldonnel years ago. He's a much better flyer than I am, that's why I'm flying helicopters nowadays, they're easy compared to the stuff Fergal has to manage."

"Not at all, Inspector, don't mind him. Brian is the best pilot I've ever had the pleasure to work with. And as for those damn machines with whirring blades, I wouldn't touch one. Give me two wings and at least two engines, preferably more, and I'm happy out!" Fergal retorted.

When the new arrivals had been given tea and biscuits, Fergal asked O'Neill, "So, what have we got out here today, Brian?"

"A Cessna 172 nose-dived into the bog, it seems. Three souls on board, all lost. Conditions were good. A bit breezy, but fine, and excellent visibility. The plane belongs to the flying club based here at the airport. The pilot was very experienced, or so they say, so it's a bit of a puzzle," O'Neill said.

"And what exactly is our role?" interrupted Bolger rather curtly.

"I'm hoping you will help us to secure the scene. Keep curious onlookers away, record the comings and goings, that sort of thing. And if we find anything out of place, then we'll need you to look into it, but I doubt that we will," Fergal said.

Bolger wasn't happy that he and his boss were to be reduced to crowd control, but Lyons managed to shoot him a stern look before he said any more, and he got the message.

"Well, boys and girls, let's get moving and go and earn our money," O'Neill said, putting down his empty mug on the table.

As the group walked out to the waiting helicopter, Lyons said to Bolger, "James, can you phone Sergeant Mulholland out in Clifden? See if he can organise a 4x4 and a couple of uniforms to get out to the crash site. Get the grid reference from the co-pilot and pass it on. I don't fancy doing guard dog out here all bloody day."

"Gotcha, boss, will do," he said with a smile.

Chapter Three

Sergeant Séan Mulholland, the officer in charge of Clifden Garda station, was just settling down to his third cup of tea of the day when the phone rang. Mulholland was in his late fifties, and could have retired from the force some time ago. But being a confirmed bachelor, it suited him to remain on and keep active; he enjoyed the social aspects of his work, and the small amount of status that his position in the community bestowed upon him. After so many years in the Gardaí, he knew the ropes well, and managed to avoid quite a lot of the nonsense, as he saw it, that had recently come down from headquarters as part of the 'An Garda Síochána – A Force for Change' programme dreamt up by some daft consultants at enormous expense, no doubt.

Under Mulholland's watch, his team of twelve dealt with petty crimes in the area, motor tax and insurance violations, licensing of shotguns, renewal of licenses for the various pubs in the town and the occasional serious matter, such as a murder in the vicinity, which seemed to come along with remarkable regularity every two years or so.

Mulholland treated the locals fairly, and gave them every opportunity to be compliant, and as a result didn't have to issue many summonses, which suited him rightly given the amount of paperwork that was attached to each one.

"Clifden Gardaí," he said as he answered the phone, thinking that it was typical that every time he stopped for a few minutes to have a cup of tea, the blessed thing interrupted him.

"Is that Sergeant Mulholland?" Bolger asked.

"It is. And who might this be?"

"It's Inspector James Bolger from Galway." He went on to explain the nature of his call, and the actions that he now wanted Mulholland to carry out.

"Oh, right, Inspector. Well, I'll see what I can do. I think Ferris down at the garage has a Land Rover we might be able to borrow for a few hours, and I can send Jim Dolan and Peadar Tobin out in it. Will that do ye?" Mulholland said.

"Sounds OK. But make haste, Sergeant, make haste. This is a serious matter," Bolger said and hung up.

"Make haste, indeed. Ye can damn well wait till I've finished my tea, jumped-up Johnny," Mulholland said to himself. He didn't like Bolger, or rather, he didn't like the whole graduate entry concept which he saw as the Gardaí pandering to new-fangled ideas that took no account of local circumstances or the way policing was actually carried out across the country.

* * *

The journey out west in the helicopter was noisy and uncomfortable. Despite the obvious skill of Brian O'Neill and his equally capable co-pilot, Jane Wells, the big aircraft was buffeted about in the stiff breeze and the thermals coming up off the boggy ground now that the sun had got up properly.

The crash site had been given a name – Site Alpha – to assist in communications between the coastguard, the Galway control tower, other aircraft in the vicinity and the IAA folks, as well as the Gardaí and other groups of interested parties.

The helicopter descended to a few hundred feet above the site and circled in a wide arc, so that the downwash from the enormous rotors wouldn't disturb the scene. O'Neill wasn't happy to actually land the big machine on the marshy ground, so he hovered it two feet above the bog while the rest of the occupants scrambled out onto the spongy surface.

Speaking over the radio on account of the extraordinary amount of noise being generated by the hovering chopper, O'Neill said, "Call us on the radio if you need us to come back, otherwise we'll be here at five o'clock to collect you. Over and out." With that, the two pilots gave the universal thumbs up sign, and the helicopter rose into the air, banking steeply away back towards the city.

The paramedics had tried to erect a temporary white tent around the front of the doomed aircraft, but the stiff breeze had carried it away, and it now rested in shreds, tangled in a clutch of nearby gorse bushes.

Bolger was sent to cordon off the site with blue and white plastic crime scene tape, while Lyons squelched her way precariously over to the wreckage.

One of the paramedics, a girl, was just backing out of the little craft, and Lyons introduced herself.

"Looks grim in there. Are they all dead?" she said.

"Yes, I'm afraid so. They were very badly injured when the plane went down. I doubt if they were conscious at all after the impact," she said.

"What will you record as the cause of death?" Lyons said.

"Multiple contusions to the head and body, and the pilot has almost been cut in half by his seat belt, as well as bashing his head on the dashboard."

"Do we have any identification?" Lyons said.

"Well, we have the passenger list from the flight plan. The pilot is a Ger Fortune. The front passenger is Fionn Devaney, and the girl is Fortune's daughter, Emma. Do you think it would be OK to get them out of here back to the morgue?" the paramedic said.

"Let me speak to the IAA guy, and we'll let you know. Will you have to take them out by helicopter?" Lyons asked.

"Probably. I can't see a land vehicle getting in here, to be honest," she said.

"OK. Give me a few minutes."

* * *

Fergal O'Dwyer and Sandra Jameson had started their investigation of the crippled aircraft. Sandra was checking all of the control surfaces – rudder, flaps, ailerons, elevators – to ascertain if there was any impediment or restrictions there, and apart from the obvious damage from the crash, she could find nothing amiss. She took several dozen photographs, including close-ups of the cables and hinges that were used to move the various parts of the plane during flight.

Fergal was concentrating on the front end of the plane. He observed that the propeller had not been turning at the point of impact, which meant almost certainly that there had been engine failure. He also noted that there was a good deal of fuel that had spilled out from the plane onto the ground surrounding the wreckage. He opened the engine cowling and started to examine the engine itself. After a few minutes, he called Lyons over to where he was standing beside the upturned plane.

"Inspector, have a look at this," he said, pointing to the side of the engine.

"What am I looking at, Fergal?"

"This is very odd. The fuel line going from the pump to the carburettor is wrong. It's clear plastic. It should be rubber with a wire braid covering it for heat insulation."

"Sorry, Fergal, I don't understand. What's the issue?"

"Oh, sorry. Well, a clear plastic pipe will heat up a lot – it passes right by the exhaust manifold which is at a very high temperature. When it heats, it can close over, or even melt altogether, starving the engine of fuel. The correct pipe is insulated against the engine heat and doesn't have that problem. No maintenance man in his right mind would fit a clear plastic pipe like that – it's madness."

"But didn't this plane fly out to Inis Mór yesterday without a problem?" Lyons said.

"Yes, it did. So, that means either the fuel pipe was changed while it was out there, or maybe, due to the fact that it was flying into the wind yesterday, the heat didn't build up so much. But today, with the wind behind it, more heat built up in the engine compartment and caused the problem. I don't know to be honest," O'Dwyer said.

"So, whichever is the case, you're saying that the engine was tampered with? The plane didn't just run out of fuel?" Lyons said.

"No. There's lots of fuel spilled all around here. That's what you can smell, so there's no issue there. But we'll have to check the maintenance records back at the flying club in Galway. Something's not right, that's for sure."

"So, what happens now?" Lyons said.

"I have a good deal more checking to do, but if I may suggest that you start taking fingerprints from the engine cowling and round about just in case," O'Dwyer said.

"I don't have any of that kit with me, I'm afraid. But I can call Galway and get a forensic team out if you think that's what's needed?"

"I think, Inspector, that would be a very good idea."

Chapter Four

Lyons could hardly believe her eyes when she looked up at the sound of a strange noise wafting across the bog on the breeze. An old red tractor – belching out pale blue smoke and towing a flat-bed trailer – was crawling its way towards them, driven by an old guy in a flat cap. Seated on the trailer, one on each side, with their legs dangling over the edge, were Garda Jim Dolan and Garda Peadar Tobin.

The old tractor wheezed up to where Lyons was standing, and the two Gardaí hopped down, scrambling through the wet bog to the front of the old vehicle.

"Thanks a million, Patsy. Can you hold on a few minutes here till we see if anyone needs a lift back to the track?" Dolan asked the old man.

"Sure, of course I can. I've nothing else to be doing anyway. Take your hour," Patsy replied.

Patsy shut down the engine on the old tractor, which Lyons thought may have been a mistake as she wasn't sure, by the look of it, that it could ever be got going again.

"Good morning, Inspector," Dolan said, walking over to the drier patch on which Lyons was standing.

"Morning, Jim; Peadar. Is this your latest Garda vehicle out in these parts?" she said, unable to keep a wry smile off her face.

"Ah, no. We had Ferris's Land Rover, but it got stuck in the bog as soon as we left the old cart track, so Patsy here came to our rescue. Do you want him to hang around in case we need to get stuff brought back to the road?" Dolan said.

"Yes, OK. Inspector Bolger has been onto Galway and we're getting Sinéad Loughran out to do some forensic work on the plane. She may need a lift from the track. Is that OK?" Lyons said.

"Sure, he's in no hurry. I'll ask him to wait around for a while."

"Then, can you and Peadar take over control of the perimeter? Although I don't think we'll be too bothered with onlookers here, it's better to be safe than sorry. Inspector Bolger and I are going back to Galway with the IAA folks as soon as they're finished. The inspector isn't happy about something he's found on the plane," Lyons said.

"Oh, is foul play suspected, Inspector?" Dolan said.

"Perhaps. We'll know more later. Get things set up here, will you? I have to try and call back to Mill Street, if I can get a signal."

Lyons couldn't get her phone to produce even one bar of signal. It was hardly surprising as they were essentially in the middle of nowhere with no sign of a mast anywhere in sight. Sandra Jameson, the IAA girl, saw that

Lyons was having difficulty with her phone and walked over to her.

"Here, use this," she said, extending a rather bulky device with a short stubby aerial sticking out at the top of it, towards Lyons. "It's a satellite phone. Works anywhere," she said.

"Great, thanks, Sandra."

Lyons called Mill Street and got through to Detective Sergeant Sally Fahy. Fahy had been made up to sergeant as part of Superintendent Finbarr Plunkett's plan for the detective unit. She had originally been a civilian worker with the Gardaí some years earlier, but had enjoyed the work so much that she joined the force properly, and had proven to be most useful on a number of difficult cases faced by the detectives over the past few years. She was a natural choice for promotion, and she had joined Eamon Flynn at the rank of Detective Sergeant earlier in the year.

"Hi Sally, it's Maureen. I'm out at Site Alpha with this plane crash thing. I need you to find out where Ger Fortune lives and get out there to break the bad news to his wife. Mr Fortune and his daughter, Emma, have both been killed in the crash. Take someone with you who can stay with the family," Lyons said.

"Oh, OK, boss. I guess it's pretty grim out there. Do you need anything else?" Fahy said.

"Yes. There was another passenger in the aircraft that also lost his life, a Fionn Devaney. He's an architect, I think. Can you find out where he lives and get Eamon to do the honours as well? We need to get to them before the news breaks. And I need you to call Sinéad Loughran. The aviation inspector wants a forensic examination of the aircraft carried out. I don't know how she'll get here, but get her to figure something out, and the sooner the better."

"Right, we're on it. That's a funny number you're calling from. Can I reach you back on it?" Fahy said.

"I know, it's a satellite phone the aviation inspectors lent me, there's no signal out here on any of our mobiles. Look, when you've been to the Fortunes, call me back on it, will you? I may need you to meet me at Galway airport to do some interviews," Lyons said.

"Fine, no problem. I'd better get moving – this kind of news travels fast in these parts," Fahy said.

"Right. Talk later."

Lyons gave the phone back to Sandra Jameson, explaining that there might be a call coming in on it for her a bit later on.

"How are you getting on?" Lyons asked.

"There's not much more we can do out here. Fergal wants to arrange to get the wreckage back to Galway. He thinks the coastguard helicopter may be able to carry it out to a road, and put it on a low loader for road transport back to the airport," Jameson said.

"Really? Would the helicopter be able to lift it?" Lyons said in surprise.

"It should do. It's only about seven hundred kilos, and that thing can lift three tonnes, but it will be a tricky manoeuvre. Fergal has already been talking to Captain O'Neill about it," Jameson said.

"What about the bodies?" Lyons said.

"They're going to be taken back in the helicopter. They're bringing out three body bags shortly, and then they'll be taken back to the regional hospital. There will be a post-mortem arranged. It's more dignified than putting them on the back of the trailer and taking them by road. Can you get someone to stay here overnight? We don't think we'll be able to arrange the removal of the plane till tomorrow," Jameson said.

"Hmm, I'm not sure. It's pretty hostile terrain out here, and there's no cover of any kind. If it starts raining, it could be pretty miserable. We can't even get a vehicle here other than the old tractor. Do you think it's important to have it guarded?"

"You'd be amazed how resourceful some souvenir hunters can be, Inspector. But I see what you mean about the locale. I'll have a chat with Fergal – maybe it will be OK to leave it alone overnight, as long as you can get someone here early in the morning," Jameson said.

* * *

The remainder of the afternoon went quickly. The inspectors from the Irish Aviation Authority finished making detailed notes and taking what seemed like hundreds of photographs of the stricken plane. The three bodies were removed in the helicopter, and Sinéad Loughran had caught a lift in it on the outward journey, arriving with one of her team to carry out a detailed forensic examination of the scene.

Under the direction of Fergal O'Dwyer, Loughran and her assistant took fingerprints from all around, and the piece of plastic pipe that was considered to be material to the investigation was removed from the aircraft carefully and bagged up.

"I'd like to know everything that there is to know about this piece of tubing, Ms Loughran," O'Dwyer said.

"If you can find out who made it, where it was sourced, how old it is, who has handled it, what was used to cut it to this precise length, and anything you can get from the clips that were used to secure it, all the better," he said in a sombre tone. "I'll draw off a sample of the fuel too, and maybe you could have it analysed for impurities, especially water. You'd be surprised at how many amateur pilots don't bother to check the tanks before take-off, and condensation can mix with the fuel and cause issues."

"OK, sir. When we get back to the lab, I'll sort all that out," Loughran said.

"No need for formality, call me Fergal. And you are?" the inspector said.

"Sinéad, Sinéad Loughran. I'm the forensic team lead attached to the Detective Unit. Nice to meet you, Fergal," Loughran said.

"Yes, likewise. It's just a shame it's under such awful circumstances. But I suppose this is kind of normal for you," O'Dwyer said.

"Well, it's not usually an aircraft, but we do get to see some pretty terrible stuff. I'm sure you do too," Loughran said.

"Not all of our investigations involve fatalities, but when there are, it can be pretty grim all right. Anyway, must get on," he said, turning back towards the plane.

At 5:30, all that could have been done at Site Alpha had been completed, and the helicopter made its final journey for the day carrying the entire crew back to Galway airport.

When they arrived back, Lyons asked everyone to wait for a few more minutes as she set out the plan for the following day. When this had been done, she walked back to her car with James Bolger.

"I need you to get out to Inis Mór first thing and interview everyone who was at the airstrip yesterday when the Fortunes took off, James," Lyons said.

"How am I going to get out there at that hour of the morning, Maureen?" Bolger asked.

"Christ, James, did they not teach you anything at all in that university of yours? And by the way, it's Inspector or Boss, OK?"

"Yes, sorry, boss. But the question remains, how am I going to get there?"

"There are scheduled flights from Inverin. Or you could get a boat, or failing that you could swim out there. Just get there and do the interviews with the airport people, use your initiative!" she said.

They travelled back to the Garda station in Mill Street in silence.

Chapter Five

As Ger Fortune's prosperity increased, he had, like many other well-to-do trades people from Galway, built a large house for himself and his family out at Keeraun, just four kilometres from Galway city centre. Sites, and planning permission, had been readily available, and several large one-off houses now graced the narrow little roads in the area.

Fahy turned her Ford Focus in between the solid granite pillars, and drove up along the curved driveway. The front garden was composed largely of a vast expanse of neatly cut grass, bordered by granite edging stones. A few small trees punctuated the grass here and there, but these were clearly young, and probably recently planted. The house was a large double-fronted affair, with a sizeable bay window to the left of the front door. The bay construction continued up the front of the building to what Fahy presumed was the master bedroom above. Further to the left, a single-story orangery had been erected, with glass walls atop a two-foot brick base all around, and a slated roof. Much decorative wrought ironwork adorned the orangery, and a vine could be seen growing inside, trained onto wires as it spread upwards.

The roof of the house was steeply pitched, giving a sort of Hansel and Gretel appearance to the building, though it was much larger than anything to be found in nursery rhymes. The entire house was painted in a pale green-grey colour, with the woodwork around the windows and the front door coloured shiny black in contrast.

"It's well for some," she said to Garda Mary Costelloe, the uniformed officer that Fahy had brought with her, who had some experience in consoling families of the deceased.

Fahy's car crunched over the loose gravel as she turned it in the wide circle provided in front of the house. No other vehicles were in evidence, although there was a large double garage standing off well to the right of the main building that could have housed a few cars.

The two Gardaí got out and rang the bell, which was fashioned in the form of a Victorian bell pull in polished brass. Fahy heard the unmistakeable tinkle deep inside the house.

A few minutes elapsed, and the two officers thought that perhaps there was no one at home, but just as they were about to leave, the door opened noiselessly. A slim woman in her mid-forties with impeccable make-up, dressed in a very expensive light tan two piece knitted outfit, and with scraped back blonde hair tied off in a short pony tail, appeared in the opening.

"Yes, can I help you?" the woman said in a totally nondescript, slightly posh accent.

"Mrs Fortune?" Fahy said.

"Yes, I'm Barbara Fortune. What can I do for you?" she said standing firm in the doorway.

"I'm Detective Sergeant Sally Fahy, and this is my colleague Garda Mary Costelloe, may we come in please, Mrs Fortune?" Fahy said.

"Well, it's not very convenient right at this moment, I'm just on my way out," she said.

"It's quite important, Mrs Fortune, we really would appreciate a few minutes of your time," Fahy said, trying not to lose patience with the obdurate woman.

Barbara Fortune said nothing, but turned away and walked back inside her house leaving the front door open. The two Gardaí looked at each other and followed her inside. The hall of the house was tiled in a black and white diamond pattern. On the right-hand side, an ornate wooden staircase with a solid polished mahogany bannister rail, finished in a monkey tail, curved up in a wide arc to the landing above. A Turkey red carpet, with an intricate pattern in navy and gold, adorned the stairs.

Mrs Fortune had gone into the room to the right of the hallway, and the two followed her in. They entered a large drawing room, lavishly furnished, with two three-seater sofas facing each other in front of a large marble fireplace. At the back of the room a substantial mahogany sideboard was resting against the wall, with a number of brightly polished silver ornaments on its top. In the corner, a half-glazed china cabinet stood, displaying a large collection of cut crystal glassware sparkling in the afternoon sunshine that was pouring in through the side window of the room.

Mrs Fortune gestured to the two women to be seated on one of the sofas, and as they took their places, they couldn't help but feel like a couple of candidates for a job interview, such was the presence of the woman of the house.

"What's all this about?" Mrs Fortune asked tersely.

Fahy was first to speak.

"Mrs Fortune, may I ask where your husband is today?"

Barbara Fortune rolled her eyes to heaven. "Gadding about in that silly little aeroplane of his somewhere, I suppose. Why, what's he done?"

"Would he have gone out to the Aran Islands perhaps?" Fahy said, feeling her way gently into the conversation.

"Yes, I think so. He's with that terrible bore Devaney, and our daughter of course, Emma. She follows him round like a puppy. It's pathetic," the woman said, looking away into space.

"I'm sorry to tell you, Mrs Fortune, but a light aircraft with three people on board was involved in an accident on its way back from Inis Mór this morning. Do you happen to know the registration of the plane?" Fahy said.

"Accident? What kind of accident?" Barbara Fortune said, wringing her hands together as she sat on the edge of her seat.

"I'm afraid it was very serious. None of the occupants survived the crash. We have reason to believe that the plane may have been carrying your husband, your daughter, and Mr Devaney," Fahy said.

The two Gardaí paused, waiting for some kind of reaction or emotional outburst from the woman sitting opposite, but none came.

After a few moments of tense silence, Barbara Fortune eventually spoke.

"I see. Are you certain no one survived?" she said.

"I'm afraid that is correct, Mrs Fortune. Is there someone you can call to be with you?" Mary Costelloe said.

"That won't be necessary. I'm going out shortly in any case. I have to be in Dublin later on."

Sally Fahy was quite surprised at the reaction, or lack of it, from the bereaved woman. There were no tears, no hysterics, just a cold deadpan look in the woman's eyes. Fahy pressed on.

"We'll need you to come in and identify the bodies, Mrs Fortune, but tomorrow will be fine. We can send a car for you."

"No, I'm afraid that won't be possible. I'll be in Dublin, I just said. You'll have to get someone else to identify them. I'll be busy."

Fahy assumed that the news they had given the woman simply hadn't sunk in. She had seen this kind of reaction before. It would probably hit her later in the day, and then she would become inconsolable with grief.

"Perhaps it might be best to postpone your trip to Dublin, Mrs Fortune, under the circumstances. Mary here can stay with you until you get someone to come around. Have you any close relatives nearby?" Fahy said.

"I don't need you to tell me how to live my life, Sergeant. As I have said, I'm driving to Dublin in a few minutes, so if that's all, I'd like you both to leave," Mrs

Fortune said, standing up and expecting the two Gardaí to do the same.

Fahy was used to bad news being received in various different ways, but she had never witnessed anything like this. She had no idea how to handle it, except to give Mrs Fortune her business card, and ask the woman for her contact details. Barbara Fortune reeled off a mobile phone number, and Mary Costelloe jotted it down. Then the two Gardaí were bundled out of the house in short order.

"Jeez, what did you think of that?" Costelloe said as they got back into Fahy's car.

"Ah, don't mind her. She could just be in shock. She'll probably dissolve in a heap in an hour's time and have to stop on the road and call someone," Fahy said. "Let's get back to the station."

Chapter Six

Back at Mill Street, Lyons arranged a briefing with her team before they all went their separate ways for the night.

Superintendent Mick Hays, Lyons' partner in life, had heard about the plane crash, and when he was told that they were all back at the station, he came down from his office on the third floor and walked the few paces to where the detectives had been set up in another building by the Office of Public Works, their own station being full to capacity. Hays let himself in, and sat at the back of the open-plan room where the briefing was taking place.

Lyons acknowledged his arrival with a nod; she was standing at the top of the room beside the whiteboard.

"OK. This is what we have so far." She went on to explain what they had discovered out at Site Alpha, and the surprise that the IAA inspector had found in the engine compartment of the stricken aircraft.

"When Sally and Mary went out to break the news to Mrs Fortune, she didn't seem too bothered, according to Sally. So, I'm not sure what's going on there, but we need to find out. Sally, tomorrow morning will you start digging on Barbara Fortune and see what you can get?"

"Sure, boss. Can I rope John in for some help?"

Garda John O'Connor was the squad's techy guy. He loved exploring mobile phones and computers, revealing secrets that would otherwise have remained hidden from the detectives. He had developed some interesting skills in this area too, and there was no device that he couldn't hack, if there was a need.

"Yes, of course. And if you find anything, let me know at once. Don't wait for the next briefing."

"James, you're going to swim out to Inis Mór first thing. I want everyone who was at the airport out there interviewed, and then you can go to the hotel where they stayed overnight and interview all of them as well. Don't leave anyone out, and get contact details for all the other guests that were there the night the Fortunes stayed over too," Lyons said.

"Can I take someone with me, boss?" He was obviously a quick learner.

"Take Mary – she's a good swimmer, or so I hear! Ask her to wear her own clothes – we don't want to scare the natives. Oh, and James – remember she's not your lacky just because she's a lower rank. Treat her with respect and give her meaningful things to do," Lyons said.

"Of course, boss. As if," Bolger said, looking slightly offended at the suggestion.

"Eamon, what did you find out when you went to see the architect's wife – Devaney, is it?" Lyons said.

"A very different story to Mrs Fortune, that's for sure. She was a mess basically. Totally destroyed by the news. I had to get her sister over to stay with her. She didn't like

Ger Fortune much either, and as for that plane, she hated it when Fionn had to go up in it," Flynn said.

"Anything specific about Fortune?" Lyons asked.

"She was too upset to be coherent, boss. But I think it might be worth having another word when she's calmed down. I got the feeling there's more to tell," Flynn said.

This was typical of Eamon Flynn. He had a nose for information – especially when it was somewhat reluctantly given – and he was known for his tenaciousness. He often worried away at a witness long after everyone else had lost interest, only to reveal some vital clue that sometimes helped to solve a difficult case. Lyons was happy to let him at it.

"OK. Well, when you think the time is right, follow that up with her, but don't harass her," Lyons said. "Anything interesting about the daughter?"

"Not so far. Just a poor teenager in the wrong place at the wrong time as far as I can see. Very sad," Flynn said.

"But remember what Mrs Fortune said about her following her father round like a puppy," Sally Fahy said.

"Normal teenage behaviour, I'd say. Did you get the impression there was anything more to it, Sally?" Lyons asked.

"Maybe a bit of jealousy – you know – mother not getting enough attention. Daughter apple of daddy's eye, that sort of thing," Fahy said.

"Mmm, OK, well, keep it in mind when you go digging. Oh, and Eamon, could you find the headteacher of her school too? I know they're on holidays just now, but he needs to be told, and he'll have some way of advising the rest of the kids in her class. Right, plans for tomorrow then. Sally, James – you two are already assigned. I'm going out to the airport here in the morning, and I'll take Liam Walsh with me. We need to interview the maintenance folks that looked after the plane, and anyone else of interest. I'll give Fergal O'Dwyer a call and co-ordinate with him. And before we head out there, I'll talk to Sinéad, see if she's got anything from the bits and pieces she took away from the scene. That's all for now, have a good evening everyone."

Liam Walsh was the final new recruit to the Galway Detective Unit. He was young, and had been chosen from the ranks of the uniformed Gardaí by Hays after he had done some background checks. By all accounts, the young man was very keen, and had impressed his superiors with his natural aptitude for the job already, although he had been in the force for just over a year.

As the room thinned out, Hays came over to where Lyons was packing up her bag.

"How did I do?" she asked him.

"Great, as usual. You know I'm not scrutinizing you, Maureen, it's just an interesting case, that's all," he said, trying to reassure her.

"Hmm. So, what's your take on it?" she said in a slightly prickly tone. Although she had been responsible for the resolution of several difficult cases since she joined the Detective Unit in Galway, Maureen Lyons still had some doubts about herself and her abilities.

"It could be a triple murder from what you have discovered so far. Pretty nasty stuff. What I'd like to know is who was the intended victim. It was hardly all three of them," Hays said.

"My money's on Ger Fortune, unless someone was pissed off with Fionn Devaney over a house design that turned out a mess. But that's hardly a reason to kill him and another two to boot," Lyons said.

"So, who have you got to investigate Mr Fortune then?" Hays said.

"I was going to keep him for little old me. But if you have some spare time, you could lend a hand?" Lyons said.

Hays checked to see that all the others had left the room, then he put his arms around Lyons and drew her close.

"I could be persuaded, I guess," he said with a mischievous grin.

"OK. Let's get home and I'll persuade you, but first – food. I'm starving!"

* * *

Over the meal in one of their favourite restaurants in Galway city – O'Connaire's down by the docks – conversation turned to the new arrangements that they were both now working under.

"So, how's it going upstairs?" Lyons asked as she tucked into a large bowl of seafood chowder and buttered a slice of homemade granary bread.

"So-so. I wasn't aware that the entire force was run on spreadsheets. I have about two hundred of the damn things covering everything from Garda overtime to clear-up rates. God only knows if anyone actually reads them. What about you?" Hays said.

"Pretty good, thanks. The team are getting on well together. We'll get Mary properly set up shortly, and it's too early to make any judgement on Liam, but I'll see what happens over the next month or so. Eamon doesn't seem to be too peeved; if anything, it's sharpened his focus, although he's not wild about Bolger," Lyons said.

"How do you rate the boy wonder?"

"A bit early to tell about him too, but unless I'm mistaken, somewhere behind all the fake tan, leather jacket and hair gel lies a half-decent detective. It just needs someone to bring it out of him."

"No one better than Senior Inspector Lyons for that job, I'd say."

"Flattery, Superintendent, will get you everywhere."

Chapter Seven

It was a lovely summer morning when Lyons collected Liam Walsh at Mill Street Garda Station soon after nine o'clock. They battled with the normal heavy morning traffic on their way out to the airport beyond Ballybrit.

"How do you want to play this, boss?" Walsh asked as they edged along at a snail's pace.

"We'll find the manager of the flying club. He's been told to expect us, so he should be there. Fergal O'Dwyer, the inspector from the IAA will be joining us too. I'd like us both to conduct the interviews. We need to see the maintenance guys as well, and anyone else that comes up in the conversation. I'll lead, but feel free to come in any time you like, and watch the body language very carefully. We may learn more from what is not said, than what is," she said.

When they turned off the main road, they followed the signs to the Atlantic Flying Club, and drove in through a set of open chain link gates. Lyons noticed that although there was a small hut where a security guard might have been posted, none was present. Lyons turned her car to the right, and pulled up in front of a large double portacabin with an Atlantic Flying Club sign affixed to it. Nearby, on the concrete apron, two smart looking Cessna 172 aircraft stood side by side.

Lyons and Walsh entered the office, and were greeted by the sole occupant.

"Good morning, officers. My name is Charlie Willis. I'm the manager of the club. Come in and take a seat," the man said, gesturing to two office chairs placed in front of his wooden desk.

Willis was a shortish, slim man, standing at around five foot eight inches. He was dressed in a pilot's sleeveless white shirt, with black epaulets bearing four gold stripes on a black background on each shoulder, dark trousers and well-polished black leather shoes. Lyons judged him to be in his early fifties, although his thinning hair and almost bald pate may have exaggerated his years. He spoke in a neutral British accent.

"We're very sorry for your recent loss, Mr Willis. It's very tragic. I'm sorry to bother you at this time, but we need to look into certain matters concerning the accident. Maybe you could start by telling us a little about the club here?" Lyons said.

Lyons was just marking time till O'Dwyer joined them, but she was interested in the background to the flying club too.

"As you know, Inspector, commercial flights to Galway have been stopped now for over a year. Apparently, they weren't viable, and when the Public Service Obligation subsidy was cut by the government, the airlines on the route pulled out altogether. So now, it's just us and the coastguard, and whatever other private aviation that comes and goes. It's quite handy in some ways, because we have the place more or less to ourselves, and we get quite a bit of charter work too," Willis said.

Outside, Lyons heard another car pulling up, and a moment later Fergal O'Dwyer and Sandra Jameson entered the small office. Introductions were made all around, and the two new arrivals sat down on the only two remaining chairs.

"We noticed, Mr Willis, that there is no security at the gate here, and that the place is more or less open to the four winds. Is that the way it normally is?" Liam Walsh asked when there was a brief lull in the conversation.

"Yes, that's right, officer," Willis said, "the club has very limited funds, and we can't afford a security presence. We do have a company that patrols once or twice a night in a van, but that's as much as we can manage. I'm the only fully paid person on the staff."

"What about the maintenance people?" Fergal O'Dwyer asked.

"They are all volunteers. We have some very keen members – all properly certified, of course. Many of our members have had a long career in aviation in various roles. We have a number of retired airline pilots, and quite a few engineers too. It's a very active club," Willis said.

"I'll need to get a list with names and addresses for all your members," Lyons said, nodding to Liam Walsh.

"Of course. That's not a problem," Willis said.

"And what about the maintenance records for Alpha Tango, Mr Willis?" Sandra Jameson said.

Willis said nothing, but turned around in his seat and reached for a lever arch file with the letters EI-XAT

41

written in broad black marker along its spine. He retrieved the heavy folder, and turned back to the audience.

"All in here, Ms Jameson, and all bang up to date. Alpha Tango was in top class condition, as are all of our aircraft. I wouldn't have it any other way."

"Are you a certified engineer yourself, Mr Willis?" Jameson said.

"I am indeed. I'm ex-RAF. Served for fifteen years in Godalming, Surrey. I've worked on everything from Spitfires to European Fighter Jets and everything in between, in my time. And I've done some work for the British Air Accident Investigation Bureau too," Willis said with obvious pride.

"How have you ended up here, Mr Willis?" Liam Walsh said.

"Ah, a familiar story, I'm afraid. I fell for the charms of an Irish civilian worker at the base, and she persuaded me to move back to her home country four years ago. We got married here in Galway, and I've never looked back since."

Fergal O'Dwyer shuffled uneasily in his seat.

"Mr Willis, you'll be familiar with the fuel supply system on the Cessna 172, then?" O'Dwyer said.

"Yes, of course, every inch of it."

"So what type of fuel line would you expect to see running between the carburettor and the fuel pump on one of those?" O'Dwyer went on.

"FAA certified rubber hose with an overlay of braided aluminium for heat dissipation, crimped at both ends is what we use. That's in accordance with the engine manufacturer's specification," Willis said.

"So, you wouldn't expect to find clear plastic tubing held on by Jubilee clips in there then?" O'Dwyer pressed on.

"Certainly not. That would be very foolish indeed. Clear plastic tube heats up and could easily close over, or melt altogether, starving the engine of fuel, or causing a fire. Why do you ask?" Willis said indignantly.

"Would you mind if Sandra here went and had a look inside the engine bay of your other two machines?" O'Dwyer said, gesturing to the window through which the two Cessnas could clearly be seen.

"Of course not. Go ahead, Ms Jameson. You'll find everything in order, I promise you."

Sandra Jameson got up and left the portacabin to walk the short distance to where the two aircraft were parked. Liam Walsh, sensing an almost imperceptible signal from Lyons, joined her.

"So, who exactly would have been the last person to work on Alpha Tango, Mr Willis?" O'Dwyer asked.

"I'll have to consult the log," he said, opening the large black folder, and thumbing through the pages.

"Yes, here we are. That would have been Terry Normoyle. He did the one-hundred-hour engine service on her just over a week ago, and I inspected the work and signed it off when he had finished. Terry is an ex Aer Lingus engineer, now retired, and one of our most reliable volunteers," Willis said.

"And is there anything in the record about changing a fuel line, Mr Willis?" O'Dwyer said.

Willis examined the two pages describing the work done.

"No, nothing. Engine oil changed, oil filter changed, spark plugs cleaned and adjusted, fuel filters blown out, electrics checked for correct voltage, battery inspected. That's it. Look, check it yourself," Willis said turning the folder around for O'Dwyer to examine. Fergal O'Dwyer studied the pages carefully, and nodded.

"Yes, that all seems to be in order, Mr Willis. I'll need to take a copy of this entire folder away with me. Can you arrange that?" O'Dwyer said.

"Yes, of course, but it will take me an hour or two to do the copying. Our machine here isn't that quick. May I ask what your interest in the fuel system of Alpha Tango is?" Willis asked.

O'Dwyer looked at Lyons, who nodded back at him.

"Mr Willis, preliminary examination of the engine bay of the crashed plane revealed that the fuel line between the carburettor and the fuel pump had been replaced with a clear plastic tube, and affixed with Jubilee clips at both ends. We believe that may have been the cause of the accident: as you say, the pipe may have heated up and closed over, starving the engine of fuel."

Lyons watched carefully for the reaction that she knew would come from the Englishman.

"Good God. But how did that happen? It must have been done when the plane was parked out on Inis Mór overnight. No one here would ever fit that rubbish to one of our planes," Willis said indignantly.

And as Lyons watched Charlie Willis, she saw the inevitable dawning of the consequences of the switch in the fuel line on his face.

"So... you think it may have been deliberate?" Willis said, noticeably paler.

Chapter Eight

James Bolger and Mary Costelloe had elected to take the ferry from Rossaville to Inis Mór. Neither of them was particularly keen on going by air, although the flight from Inverin to the island was only ten minutes long, and it was a commercial operation, so they assumed quite rightly that safety would be paramount. In any case, the longer ferry journey would give them a chance to discuss how they wanted to conduct the interviews once they got to their destination.

It was a fine morning for the ferry ride. The boat, named "Grá na Farraige", or "Love of the Sea" was a fine vessel that cut through the gentle swell that was ever present on the Atlantic coast. Catering on board, although limited, was surprisingly good, and the two Gardaí soon settled down with freshly brewed coffee and pastries in the interior lounge where it was peaceful, most of the other passengers having opted for the outdoor seating on the upper deck to take full advantage of the scenery.

"So, Mary, how long have you been a detective then?" Bolger asked by way of making conversation with the pretty young Garda with jet black hair and tantalising green eyes.

"I'm just transferring at the moment. I've been in uniform for three years, but when the chance to transfer to the detective unit came up, I grabbed it. The work is much more interesting. What about you, Inspector?" she said.

"You'd better call me James for the day. We don't want to frighten the natives with too much police talk," Bolger said, smiling a slightly cheesy smile.

"Very well, James, so what's your story?"

"I'm one of these experiments, Mary. The Gardaí has to modernise you see. Catch up with the rest of Europe with new policing methods. So that means taking in recruits who have come through a different channel from the norm. I'm one of the first of several Graduate Entry Inspectors. I've never been in uniform, and I've never walked the beat, or had to answer to a grumpy old Sergeant, but neither have I seen much policing up close and personal. Does that horrify you?" he said.

"Well, it's very different. If you compare it to Inspector Lyons. She started off in uniform. She apprehended a bank robber in Galway city centre one day when she was on the beat, almost by accident, and then went on to become Detective Sergeant and Inspector, before taking over Hays' role as Senior Inspector. She has loads of experience with murder, kidnapping, robbery and all sorts. And she's been shot at," Mary Costelloe said, as if this was in her view the ultimate badge of honour for a member of the force.

"And does that make her a better cop than me?" Bolger said.

"Different anyway, I guess." This was as far as Mary was prepared to go, although it didn't truly reflect her true thoughts on the matter.

* * *

The ferry pulled up alongside the jetty at Inis Mór, and the skipper helped the passengers up the steps and back onto dry land. Mary Costelloe felt that they had missed an opportunity by not mixing with the rest of the people on the ferry as the journey unfolded. The plane crash would undoubtedly have been the main topic of conversation for some of the others on board at least, and they might have overheard something of value. Nevertheless, she kept her views to herself, not wanting to alienate the inspector so early on.

Making enquiries at the harbour, it wasn't long before James Bolger and Mary Costelloe arranged a lift from the jetty out the one and a half kilometres to the small airport on the island.

"That was a fierce accident yesterday with that poor man and his daughter," the driver said, keen to make conversation with the two strangers.

"Yes, indeed it was. There were three of them in the plane you know," Costelloe said, anxious to make up for the earlier mistake of not communicating with the locals.

"I heard that, all right. That builder fellow, his daughter and the architect. I suppose that'll put an end to the plans for a big hotel then," the driver said.

"Well, maybe. We'll see. Were you hoping it would go ahead?" Costelloe said.

"Ah sure, what does it matter to me? But there was a good few that were against it all the same. Too many tourists already out here, some would say," he said, looking in the rear-view mirror to judge the reaction of his two passengers seated in the back of his old Toyota.

"So, there was a bit of opposition to the idea then?" Costelloe pressed on.

"Ah, mostly all hot air. There's some folks always complaining about something, don't ye know. So, what has you two out here anyways?" the driver asked, unable to get the information he sought indirectly.

Bolger was about to speak, but Mary Costelloe nudged him and said quickly, "We're just out to see about a sightseeing trip around the islands. James here is interested in nature," she said, but of course the driver didn't believe her.

"Oh, right so, well here we are. Is this OK for you?"

"Fine thanks, how much do we owe you?" Costelloe asked.

"Ah, you're grand, sure it's only a short hop. But if you want to make a contribution for the diesel…"

Mary dug in her purse and produced a five euro note, handing it to the driver who took it gratefully and put it in his inside jacket pocket.

"Very generous, thank you ma'am," he said.

The two Gardaí got out of the old car and walked over to the only building that occupied the airport on Inis Mór. It was surprisingly busy. The morning flight from Inverin, which went on to the other two islands in the trio that made up the Aran Islands, had just arrived, and passengers were alighting and embarking. The plane that was used on the short journeys between the islands and the mainland was a Britten Norman Islander – appropriately named in this case. It could carry nine passengers in all, along with some basic freight and baggage. It was a twin-engined machine, and performed its duties reliably and safely even in some of the very poor weather that nature could produce out there from time to time.

They hung around outside the building until all the passengers had dispersed, either onto the plane, or away about their business. Inside the building, the sole occupant was in radio contact with the aircraft about to depart, giving the pilot taxiing instructions and wind readings.

"Bravo Hotel, clear for take-off runway three-two, then a right turn out to Inis Maan. Slán."

When the operator had finished on the radio, James Bolger approached him.

"Good morning, sir. My name is Inspector Bolger from the Galway Detective Unit, and this is my colleague Detective Costelloe," he said gesturing towards Mary. "We'd like to talk to whoever was on duty yesterday when Mr Fortune's plane took off from here to go to Galway," Bolger said.

"That would be me," replied the slim, tall man in a very neutral accent.

"And you are?" Bolger said.

"Station Manager Séan McCreedy."

"Thank you, Mr McCreedy. Could you just go through the events leading up to the departure of the flight yesterday for us, please?"

"There's nothing unusual to tell, officer. The plane had been parked here overnight. I think Mr Fortune and his party must have been staying at the hotel. They arrived out here mid-morning. Mr Fortune did a walk around check of the aircraft, boarded and departed. That's about it," McCreedy said.

"Except that it isn't, is it? The plane got about fifteen minutes away, and crashed into the bog and three people died," said Bolger.

McCreedy had no answer to that.

"So, tell us about the security here at the airport, Mr McCreedy," Bolger continued, feeling that he had the upper hand at this point.

"There isn't really any, to be honest, Inspector. Not much happens around here that requires security. We observe all the required checks for boarding passengers of course, baggage screening and so on, but that's about it," McCreedy said.

"What about at night? How do you secure the premises after all the flights have come and gone?" Bolger said.

"We don't. There has never been any need to try and secure the place after hours. No one would come and interfere with anything here," McCreedy said.

"So, anyone could simply walk onto the airport compound and do whatever they wanted to a plane that was parked here overnight, and no one would be any the wiser. Is that it?" Bolger said.

"But why would anyone want to do anything like that?" McCreedy said.

"That's what we are here to try and find out, Mr McCreedy."

Mary Costelloe wasn't at all happy about the way the discussion was going. Bolger seemed to be locked into some kind of verbal battle with McCreedy, which was not the best way to get information, in her view. She managed to catch Bolger's eye, and nod towards the door. At first, he didn't get it, but when Mary repeated the gesture, he looked at her with a puzzled frown on his face, but then simply walked to the door and let himself out.

"Look, I'm sorry about the Inspector, Mr McCreedy. His heart is in the right place – he's just trying to get to the bottom of what, so far, is a right old mystery. Can I ask, have you ever had any situations where a plane was interfered with overnight, when the airport was not attended?" she said.

"No, never. It's just not that kind of place. Why, what happened to the plane?" McCreedy asked.

"Well, we're not completely sure yet, but it may have been tampered with. But there's nothing to say that it happened here. Has there been much opposition locally to Mr Fortune's plans to build a luxury spa hotel on the island?" Mary asked, changing the subject.

"Oh, you know. There are some of the locals who don't want change – any change – at any cost. They can be quite vocal, but they're harmless. They'd never get involved in anything like that," McCreedy said.

"Is there anyone in particular that has strong views about Fortune's plans?"

"Well, I know Martin McGettigan isn't too happy about it. He runs the only hotel currently on the island, and Fortune's plans could threaten his business. But he's a very decent man. I can't see him actually doing anything about it other than grumble a bit to some of the locals in the bar."

"OK, thanks, Mr McCreedy. Look, if I give you my card, can you get in touch with me if anything else comes to mind, or if there's any gossip that might have a bearing on the case?" Costelloe said.

"You want me to spy on the locals for you, is that it?"

"No, well not exactly, but we need all the help we can get on this one, and don't forget, three people died in that plane crash, including a seventeen-year-old girl," Costelloe said, tilting her head slightly to one side and flashing her bright green eyes at the man while extending her business card in his direction.

"Very well. Thanks. But you'd better keep the Rottweiler at home next time. I don't want him in here again chucking his weight around."

"Thank you, Mr McCreedy, you've been very helpful," Costelloe said, and went outside to join the inspector.

Bolger was in a grumpy mood.

"Get anything?" he said tersely.

"Well, just that there's a Martin McGettigan that runs the hotel here who wasn't too happy about Ger Fortune's plans, for obvious reasons."

"Hmph. Right. Let's go."

Chapter Nine

Sandra Jameson inspected the two other Cessna 172 aircraft belonging to the club carefully. She was very used to this particular type of plane as it was the light aircraft favoured by flying clubs all over the country. As she walked around the aircraft, she pointed out the various parts to Liam Walsh who took it all in enthusiastically. Apart from the fact that the tyre on the nosewheel of one of the machines was wearing a bit thin, she could find nothing out of place on either of them. She wished that all the planes that she had inspected over her years with the IAA were in as good condition.

When she returned to the office of the flying club, Charlie Willis was busy feeding pages from Alpha Tango's maintenance log slowly through the photocopier.

"Those aircraft seem to be in immaculate order, Mr Willis. I'm sure you know that the nosewheel on the one nearest to us will shortly be due for replacement, but other than that, they are in excellent condition," Jameson said.

"Yes, Inspector, we have the new tyre in stock, and it will be replaced well within the serviceable hours, don't worry," Willis said.

"What's happening with Alpha Tango?" Jameson said to O'Dwyer.

"I've just been on the phone making arrangements to have the Coastguard chopper lift it onto a lorry and bring it back here. Mr Willis has said we can put it in the maintenance hangar for now. Then we'll see if we can re-construct its final moments using the instrumentation on board and the radio transcripts," O'Dwyer said.

"Will you be going back out to Site Alpha to oversee the lift?" Lyons said.

"Yes, we will. We need to make sure any loose debris is collected up, and I want to look for more traces of the instance of impact, so I can judge the angle of approach, that sort of thing. Have you any news from the forensic people about the fuel pipe?" O'Dwyer said.

"Not yet. Liam, please go with Mr O'Dwyer and Ms Jameson when they go back out to the site, just to make sure all our evidence requirements are met, and our stuff is tidied away. One of the Clifden Garda should be there by now too," Lyons said.

"Right, boss. Do you want me to stay out there?" Walsh said.

"Well, you can stay till the plane is on the lorry. Then maybe you should come back in with it, make sure no one meddles with it on route. If there was foul play, we don't want anyone thinking they can cover their tracks at this stage. I'm going back to the station to follow up on the forensics. I'll call you if I get anything, Mr O'Dwyer." Lyons said.

"Thanks, Inspector. And thanks for your help," O'Dwyer said.

* * *

Back at the office, Lyons called through to Sinéad Loughran.

"Hi Sinéad, it's Maureen. Just wondering if you found anything out about the plane crash?"

"Oh, hi Maureen. Yes, we did. There was no joy on the fingerprints. We lifted a few sets from around the engine cowling, but I haven't had a chance to check them with the people out at the flying club yet. None of them are known to us – there's nothing in the database in any case. But I had a bit more luck with the piece of tubing," Loughran said.

"Go on."

"We were lucky there. It had a maker's name printed along the side, so we contacted them and they told us that particular type is often sold into the home brewing and wine making industry. They could tell from the batch number that it was manufactured last year, but that's all. They don't know where it went – they deal with several distributors who take it," Loughran said.

"Did you by any chance ask them if it was certified for use in connection with engine fuel supplies?" Lyons asked.

"Yes, I did. They say they do make a product that can be used in automotive fuel systems, but not this one. The product we pulled from the plane is certified for general, food and beverage use only," Loughran said.

"OK, well, that's useful information, Sinéad, thanks. Will you sort out the fingerprints with the folks out at the airport?"

"Yes, will do. What about the guy that runs the airfield out at Inis Mór?" Loughran asked.

"I'll give Bolger a call and ask him to get them and bring them back to us for comparison," Lyons said.

"Grand, let me know when you have them. Thanks, bye."

* * *

James Bolger wasn't too pleased that he had to return to the airport to collect fingerprints from McCreedy, so he decided to delegate that sensitive task to Mary Costelloe. Mary didn't have a fingerprint kit with her, but she was well able to improvise for the purpose of elimination, by getting McCreedy to place his hand around a pint glass. Then Mary lifted his prints using Sellotape, and sticking it to a sheet of clear plastic that McCreedy had in his office. She knew that this wouldn't stand up in court, but that was not what it was for. She doubted that McCreedy's prints would be found on the plane, and if they were, they could return and use the proper evidence kit at a later date.

* * *

James Bolger made his way to the only hotel on the island. It was approaching lunchtime, and he was feeling peckish from all the fresh sea air, so he decided to kill two birds with one stone, as it were. He strolled into the lounge bar of the hotel, where several of the tourists that had been on the same ferry out to the island were seated tucking into bowls of homemade soup and brown bread.

Behind the bar, a small, rather plump woman with short grey curly hair was busy serving. Bolger waited his turn, and when she eventually got to him, he asked, "Is Mr McGettigan around?"

"He's busy in the kitchen just now," the woman replied in a strong Galway accent, "you'll be the man from the police on the mainland then."

Bolger wondered for a split second how his identity had been so readily spotted, but then realised that he probably stuck out like a sore thumb, and no doubt the locals had both he and Mary Costelloe pegged from the moment they stepped onto the ferry in Rosaville.

"Yes, that's me. Could you ask him to pop out when he has a minute? I need a word. In the meantime, I'll try some of your soup and a smoked salmon sandwich if I may?" he said.

"Right enough, but Marty will be a few minutes – it's fierce busy back there at the moment, sir," the woman said, turning her attention once more to the beer taps on the bar and pulling a frothy pint of something pale.

Bolger sat up at the bar on one of the plain wooden stools, and awaited his food.

"Will you be having a drink of something, sir?" Mrs McGettigan said.

"Oh, no thanks. Not for me. I'm on duty," Bolger said. He regretted the words as soon as they had left his mouth, but it was a reflexive response that he couldn't help.

The soup and smoked salmon sandwich were exceptionally good, and James wasted no time in putting them away. As he finished the last tasty morsel, a man appeared behind the bar. He was tall, probably in his early fifties, with a full shock of greying hair and a ruddy face. He was a big man in every respect, with a sizeable paunch straining at the plain blue shirt and grey trousers that showed evidence of recent work in the kitchen.

"Detective," he boomed, "I'm Marty McGettigan. How can I help you?" he said, extending his hand across the bar.

"Ah, hello Mr McGettigan. I wonder if there's somewhere a bit quieter we could have a chat?" Bolger said.

"I'm afraid this will have to do ye. We're very busy today, and I can't leave Biddy on her own at lunchtime."

"Oh, all right. I suppose you heard about the plane crash over on the mainland yesterday?" Bolger said.

"I did. Terrible business. That poor young girl – only sixteen, was she?"

"I believe they stayed here the previous night," Bolger said.

"They did – all three of them."

"Did you get a chance to talk to them for long, Mr McGettigan?"

"Sure, what would I want to be talking to those two for? Aren't they planning to put me out of business?" McGettigan said.

"So, you weren't in favour of their development plans then?"

"Do ye think turkeys vote for Christmas?" the man said bitterly.

"Did you happen to overhear any of their conversation at all?" Bolger said.

"Look. We don't go around eavesdropping on our guests or gossiping about their business. I gave them bed and board for the night and they paid me in full, in cash. That's about it. And as for their daft scheme to turn the island into some kind of mad holiday resort – well maybe it's worked out for the best, sad and all as it is." And with that, McGettigan turned away to serve another man who was queueing for drinks further along the bar.

Just as Bolger was trying to figure out how he could get more information from McGettigan, Mary Costelloe joined him.

"Oh hi, Mary. How did you get on?" he said.

"Fine. I'll tell you later," she said, not wanting to reveal that she had been collecting fingerprints to the entire population of the bar.

"What about you? Did you get anything much here?" she asked.

"Nothing. Just a confirmation that the Fortunes and Devaney stayed here overnight. But no one is talking."

"Did you get McGettigan's prints?"

"No, should I?"

Mary Costelloe rolled her eyes to heaven, wondering how on earth James Bolger had ever qualified for police work.

"Watch and learn, sir," she said.

Mary ordered a soft drink with plenty of ice from Martin McGettigan, who obligingly presented her with it in a glass that he held in his left hand. When the opportunity arose, Mary took the drink and went with it to the bathroom where she repeated the exercise with the sticky tape to collect McGettigan's prints. She poured the sickly-sweet orange liquid away.

Back at the bar, which was now thinning out, Mary managed to get Biddy McGettigan to herself for a few moments while Bolger was having another unsuccessful go at extracting information from the woman's husband.

"Is there anyone, or any group in particular, Biddy, that you think might have had strong opposition to Fortune's plans?" Mary asked.

"Apart from my husband, you mean? To be honest, girl, there were very few on the island who were in favour of it. Oh, when Fortune was out here, there were those who licked up to him in the hope of getting some bit of work perhaps, but as soon as he was gone, they'd all congregate in the bar here and complain loudly about the whole thing. There was even talk about organising a protest group, but that never got off the ground. Do you think the whole thing will die a death now, Mary?" Biddy McGettigan said, unaware of the irony.

"Probably. I can't see anyone else likely to take it up, can you?"

"No, probably not. 'Tis a sad business, that's for sure, but you know what they say about an ill wind."

Chapter Ten

The following morning, Hays was looking forward to some operational work to get him away from the endless paperwork. He called James McMahon at his office as soon as he felt it was a respectable hour.

"James, it's Mick Hays. How are you keeping?" Hays said.

"Oh, hello, Inspector, I'm good thanks, what can I do for you?" McMahon said.

Hays chose not to correct the man concerning his newly acquired more senior rank.

"Just wondering if you might be free for a sandwich later on? There's something you might be able to help me with."

"Hmm, let's see, well, I have a meeting with a client here at twelve, but that shouldn't take long. I could meet you in the Imperial at, say, one o'clock. Can you give me a clue what it's all about?" McMahon said.

"Great, I'll see you at one then. Thanks." Hays hung up before he had to divulge any information.

Hays had come across James McMahon a few years back during an investigation into the murder of a Polish girl out on the old bog road west of Roundstone. McMahon had been seeing the girl, but wasn't involved in the crime itself. Hays had come across the architect socially on a number of occasions since, and had found him to be affable and easy to get along with, so the two had become, if not good friends, at least close acquaintances.

Hays had no difficulty filling the rest of the morning completing reports on resource usage in the team and writing a submission in support of his chief's proposal for further resources for the Western force.

At 12:45 he left the office and walked round to the Imperial Hotel on Eyre Square, bumping into his lunch date outside the hotel. The two men went in and made for the grill where they would have a more substantial meal than had been suggested in the earlier phone call.

As they ordered from the lunch menu, McMahon broke the silence, "Well, Mick. What can I do for you?"

"You'll have heard about the plane crash out west that took the lives of Ger Fortune, his daughter and Fionn Devaney," Hays said.

"Terrible business. I never liked those small planes. Give me a 737 any day, or better still, a four-engined jet," McMahon said.

"I know what you mean. Did you know Ger Fortune at all?" Hays said.

"Yes, sure. He had been a pretty big cog in the Galway building scene recently. He started building park houses way back before the crash, but moved on to more exotic stuff," McMahon said.

"Park houses?"

"Yes. House building falls into three main categories here in Galway. There are terraced houses, usually three bedroomed starter homes built in blocks of four or six in fairly large quantities on estates. Then there are the park houses. Three and four bedroomed schemes of semi-detacheds with names like Cherry Tree park, Cherry Tree avenue, crescent, rise etc. These are of a better specification than the terraced houses, and have front and back gardens. Ideal for Mr and Mrs Average. The larger houses he'd been into recently have names like The Pines, Oakdene, Crofton Glade and so on. These are four and five bedroomed detached houses with a decent sized plot. They sell for up to seven hundred thousand euro these days, and I can tell you there is no shortage of buyers. We've done designs for some of them over the past few years," McMahon said.

"We heard he was looking into some sort of hotel development out on Inis Mór. Have you heard anything about that?" Hays asked.

"That will have been Devaney's idea. He always tried to punch above his weight. To be honest, I think it was a daft scheme, but Devaney had convinced Fortune that it was a great opportunity and would make them both a pile of money," McMahon said.

"I see. Any idea how they were going to fund it?" Hays said.

"Fortune made a lot of money since the market bounced back in 2014. He was a clever man. He bought a lot of land on the cheap during the crash, and went into partnership with building contractors. I'm not sure of the details, but whatever arrangements he made were very lucrative for him. I'd say he was going to self-fund it, or maybe pre-lease it to a hotel operator like Hilton or Clayton," McMahon said.

"Hmm. I see. Nice work if you can get it. Do you think he might have had any enemies?"

"Who? Devaney or Fortune?" McMahon said.

"Either."

"Well, when the crash came, Fortune owed a lot of money to sub-contractors. I never heard the details, but the word was that he left a lot of them up the creek, and some of them took it very badly – hardly surprising. But that wasn't unusual at that time. He even left us short of a few grand too, but then so did a lot of other builders," McMahon said.

"Interesting. Any of them particularly vocal about Fortune?" Hays said.

"None you could name, but there's probably a fair bit of resentment out there for him, especially as he came out of the whole thing smelling of roses. We're not terribly comfortable with success in this city, as I'm sure you know. Anyway, why all the interest?" McMahon said.

"Ah, it's probably nothing, but there are a few aspects of the accident that have us puzzled, that's all. I can't say more for now, but it's not often that three of Galway's finest citizens die on the one day, so we're looking a bit closer at it."

"I see, interesting. If you're looking for people that might have had a grudge against Ger Fortune, it could be a long list. But surely you don't think anyone could have caused the accident somehow?" McMahon said.

"I can't say too much for now, let's just say there are some aspects of the accident that we need to investigate a bit more. I'm not involved myself, Inspector Lyons is leading the enquiry," Hays said.

"Ah, yes, I remember Ms Lyons. If there is someone behind it, God help them with Inspector Lyons on the case. How is she, anyway? Not that I am missing her or anything," McMahon said.

"She's fine. You know we are partners, don't you? We live together out in Salthill."

"I didn't know – sorry no offence intended," McMahon said.

"None taken. But you're right, Maureen is a damn fine detective. If there's anything iffy about any of this, she'll get to the bottom of it."

The waitress came and took away their empty plates, asking them if they were going to have a dessert.

Neither man wanted it, so they just ordered coffee, and sat back, now replete, to await the beverage.

"So, what about you, James? What keeps you busy these days?" Hays asked.

"We're up to our eyes with work. There's an awful lot of new development and refurbishment going on in the city, and thankfully, we seem to be getting more than our fair share of it," McMahon said.

"Excellent! Have you taken on more staff?"

"We're looking into it. If it goes on like this we will have to, or maybe consider amalgamating with one of the other smaller firms in town. To be honest, it's all getting a bit much for me just now – but it's hard to turn away work, given the trouble we saw in the business just a few years ago," McMahon said.

When the two men had finished their coffee, the conversation seemed to come to a natural end. As they got up to leave, McMahon said to Hays, "If you would like me to have a dig around, unofficially of course, amongst the trade, I could see if I could find out anything that might have been going on with Fortune, or Devaney."

"Yes, thanks. But don't go causing a stir. Just keep your ear to the ground. Let me know if anything jumps up at you," Hays said.

"OK. And thanks for lunch," McMahon said as they left the hotel and went their separate ways.

Chapter Eleven

The news of her husband's death had reached Fionn Devaney's wife, Ann, before Flynn had a chance to visit her. He had telephoned to make an arrangement to call on her, and it became clear at once that the woman was grieving. Her sister was with Ann at her home, and when he had conveyed his sympathy, Flynn asked if he could call around later in the day, after he had been to Emma's school.

There was no reason why he should have insisted on seeing the woman, but Flynn was known for his thoroughness, and in cases like this where there was suspicion about the death of several people, he needed to ensure that every angle was covered.

* * *

Eamon Flynn turned his car in through the impressive gates of St Begnet's Community Secondary School just off the Newcastle Road at the edge of the city.

The property had been acquired by the state in the early 1920s when the then owner – a British landlord – had fled, fearing for his safety in the turbulent times following the 1916 rising, the Irish Civil War and the other conflicts that eventually led to the foundation of the Irish Free State – the precursor to the current Irish Republic.

The state had gifted the manor house to a religious order, who established a school in the building to promote the Catholic ethos and provide much-needed education for the young citizens of Galway.

As Galway expanded, so did the school, and the old house was now surrounded by a series of random buildings that had appeared over the years, the latest additions being a set of six portacabins, stacked two high, and positioned to the rear of the old house.

Flynn had been surprised to find that the headmaster of the school where Emma Fortune had been a pupil, was still at work, despite the school holidays having started some two weeks earlier.

He pulled the car up on the expansive gravel patch in front of the rather austere looking main house, and got out. Donal O'Connell, the headmaster, had instructed Flynn to come right into the main house, the door of which would not be locked, and find his study that was situated behind the rather magnificent cantilevered staircase that swept around in a curve from the right-hand side of the hallway. Flynn found the polished solid mahogany door easily, knocked, and waited.

"Come," commanded an authoritative voice from within.

Flynn turned the brass handle and entered the room, feeling every bit as if he was the errant student lining up for some dastardly punishment.

O'Connell quickly put the policeman at ease though. He was a tall, thin man with little hair, a long narrow face, and black framed glasses. He was dressed in the archetypal schoolmaster's outfit of charcoal grey slacks, brown shoes and a tweed jacket, complete with leather elbow patches. His shirt, rather like the man himself, was somewhat creased with age.

"Good morning, Sergeant, come in, sit down. Nice morning, isn't it?" O'Connell said.

"Thank you. Yes, it is. This is a nice place you have here. I like this room in particular," Flynn said looking around at the shiny period furniture and rows of books in the gigantic bookcase behind the master's desk.

"Perk of the job, Sergeant. I get the best room in the house, for my sins. Now, how can I help you?"

"It's about Emma Fortune. I understand she was a pupil here."

"She still is, although obviously on holiday at the moment," O'Connell said.

"You haven't heard then? I'm sorry to say that Emma Fortune was the victim of a fatal accident when her father's plane crashed out near Inverin yesterday," Flynn said.

"Good God, no I hadn't heard, Sergeant. I've been too busy with end of term stuff here to listen to the news or read the papers. That's awful. Poor Emma. She was a very promising student too," O'Connell said.

"You knew her well then, sir?"

"Well, in a way, I suppose I did. She was in my Civics class. Very bright girl. But this is terrible. We haven't lost a pupil in all the time I've been here. I'll have to inform the rest of the staff of course, and the class too. They'll be devastated. And there's Mr Williams, Emma's form teacher. Oh, God – he's not here today, I'll have to call him."

"Was Emma a good student?" Flynn said.

O'Connell swivelled in his chair, and reached behind him where a number of old, dark green four-drawer filing cabinets stood. He opened a drawer labelled D-E-F and rooted amongst the files before withdrawing a single manila folder with Emma Fortune written in a neat hand on its cover.

O'Connell opened the folder, and read silently over a number of sheets of paper from the file.

"Yes, indeed she was, Sergeant. Some very promising examination results in her third year, and then for transition year she did a lot of voluntary work in the city, culminating in a fundraiser for the homeless that collected over a thousand euro which we gave to St Vincent de Paul. She was a model student as far as we were concerned. Her classmates will be distraught," O'Connell said, closing the file.

"I don't suppose you have a recent photograph of her in there by any chance?" Flynn asked.

"Yes, I have. We take them for the year book – she's with the rest of the class, but you can see her quite clearly. Here, I'll ring her face with red pen," O'Connell said, retrieving the black and white print from the file, marking it up and handing it over.

"Thanks, headmaster. Well, I'd better let you get on then, Mr O'Connell. May I give you my card in case anything comes up that you feel might be important?" Flynn said.

"Well, yes, I suppose so, but like what?"

"Oh, just anything at all. You never know," Flynn said, handing the other man his business card.

O'Connell stood up and walked the detective to the door.

"When do you think the funeral might be?" the headmaster said.

"I'm not sure, sir. It's not up to me. We may have to keep the bodies for a few days. There are some things that need sorting out," Flynn said.

"Is that usual in the case of an accident, Sergeant?" O'Connell said, holding the door to his study open.

"It's not unusual, but it shouldn't be too long anyway. Thanks for your help," Flynn said, and left.

* * *

It was well into the afternoon by the time Eamon Flynn reached the impressive house that had been built by the deceased architect, Fionn Devaney, out on the Tuam Road. The house was unusual in several respects. It was essentially fashioned in the form of three large interconnected rectangular blocks, each of different heights, but all having enormous floor to ceiling windows framed in black aluminium, with flat rooves. The entrance was not evident from the driveway, and it took Flynn a few minutes to locate the front door, which was in fact to the side of the property, hidden behind a faux wall that appeared to serve no other purpose than to conceal the door.

He rang the bell, and after a few minutes it was answered by a woman in her mid to late forties, smartly dressed, but looking drawn and upset. Before she got a chance to speak, Flynn introduced himself.

"Oh, you'd better come in. But please, Sergeant, don't stay for more than a few minutes, my sister is very poorly," the woman said.

"Of course. I'm sorry to have to call at all. I won't keep you for long," Flynn said.

In the lounge, Flynn was introduced to Ann Devaney, who was, as her sister had said, in a very bad way indeed. She sat on the edge of the sofa clutching a handkerchief that she continually used to dab at her tearful eyes.

Flynn sat down gingerly on one of the other armchairs.

"I'm so sorry for your loss, Mrs Devaney. I know this is a bad time, I just need to check a few things with you, if that's all right?"

Ann Devaney nodded almost slightly.

"What was your husband working on recently, Mrs Devaney?"

"He was spending almost every waking hour on that blasted hotel and resort that Ger Fortune wanted to build out on Inis Mór. He had one or two other small jobs on, but that thing seemed to take most of his time and energy. He was obsessed."

"May I just ask how things were between your husband and Mr Fortune, Mrs Devaney?" Flynn said.

"Fine," the woman replied in a trembling voice, "they were good friends as well as business partners. They got along well, but I never liked Fionn going up in that wretched plane." She started to sob loudly again.

"I know this is difficult, Mrs Devaney, but did your husband have any enemies? Anyone who he had fallen out with lately?" Flynn asked.

"No, no. You didn't know my husband, Sergeant. He was very well liked…"

"I'm sorry, yes of course. Look, I'll leave you in peace now. I'm sorry to have disturbed you. If you think of anything over the next few days that might be of interest, perhaps you could call me," Flynn said, extending another of his business cards to Mrs Devaney's sister.

Neither of the women spoke, and he let himself out, unaided, from the house.

Chapter Twelve

The following morning, Lyons had arranged a briefing for the entire team. She had asked Sinéad Loughran to attend as well, in case there was any forensic evidence from the crash site that might be helpful to the detectives. Superintendent Mick Hays had dropped in too, as he had a contribution to make following his meeting with James McMahon. As a courtesy to his rank, she asked him to go first.

Hays outlined the discussion he had had with the architect over lunch the previous day. When he had finished, Lyons said, "Right. We need to find out who might have been holding a grudge against Ger Fortune then. I'll hand out tasks at the end of the briefing."

James Bolger gave an account of his trip to the Aran Islands with Mary Costelloe, claiming the credit for the fingerprints that Mary had collected for himself, and talking up his conversations with the publican and the airport manager.

"Sinéad – anything of interest from Site Alpha?" Lyons said.

"I got some good prints from the plane around the engine cover and on some of the engine parts themselves. Oh, and we collected mobile phones from all three occupants. Emma had a backpack too, and there was a small laptop in it, so I have that as well," Sinéad said.

"Good. Well, give all that electronic stuff to John O'Connor and let him get busy with it. Mary, maybe you can help John with that. You know the drill. We're looking for any negative emails or text messages, anything that could give us a clue about who might be behind this. It's looking more and more like it was no accident," Lyons said.

The group stirred uneasily in their seats, and a low murmur went around the room.

"Right. Thanks, Superintendent, for coming in. There's no need to detain you if you need to go," she said looking at her partner.

"I'll be off then. Keep me posted, Maureen," he said.

"Of course, sir," she said, smiling warmly at him as he turned and left the room.

"Sally, you're going to follow up on Mrs Fortune. Her behaviour seems a long way off the typical grieving widow. Do some digging, and no need to be too subtle about it. I want to know what's going on there," Lyons said.

"Right, boss," Fahy said.

"Liam, can you take a couple of uniforms and get around to Fortune's office? I want you to collect his diaries, especially ones from a few years back if they are available, and see if you can find out anything to do with his dealings with sub-contractors – correspondence and so on. It might be worth taking John O'Connor with you. He can have a root in the computers."

"Are we OK to take things away, boss? Don't we need a warrant?" Walsh said.

"No time for that nonsense, Liam. If you meet any resistance just say that we're investigating a possible murder, but don't say who we think was the victim. That usually shuts them up. Call me if anyone tries to block you."

"Mmm, OK, Inspector," Walsh said.

"Eamon, can you follow up with the school? Talk to Emma's form teacher – Mr Williams, was it? Find out who Emma's close friends were. Maybe you could even get to speak to one or two of them, but go gently with that," she said.

"OK, Inspector. What will you be doing?" Flynn asked.

"I'm going back out to the airport with Inspector Bolger. We need to take prints from the manager out there and this Mr Normoyle who maintained the plane. I'd like to speak to him about the fuel line as well. James, can you call ahead and make sure they'll both be there in an hour or so, and we'll head on out?" Lyons said.

"Right, boss, will do," Bolger replied.

The room cleared as the team went about their assigned tasks, except for Mary Costelloe who hung back, rearranging the chairs and generally tidying up.

"All right, Mary?" Lyons said.

"Could I have a word, Inspector?" the young Garda said, looking around tentatively to see that they were alone in the room.

"Sure. What's on your mind?"

"Well, I probably shouldn't say anything, but off the record," she said hesitantly, "it's just that yesterday out on Inis Mór was a bit of a shambles."

"Oh? In what way?" Lyons said.

"Well, I know it's not my place to say, but Inspector Bolger didn't do too well, I thought. He rubbed everyone up the wrong way, and he didn't get any of those fingerprints either – I did that. I just thought you should know, but please don't let on I told you," Mary said.

"Of course not. That's interesting, Mary. Thanks for telling me, and mum's the word!"

* * *

Lyons and Bolger drove out to Galway airport together in Lyons' car.

"How did you get on yesterday?" Lyons asked.

"Oh, fine. You know what they're like out there – they don't give much away. But it's fair to say Fortune didn't have many fans on the island," Bolger said.

"How did Mary get on? She's quite new to all this. A bit like yourself really."

"Yes, and it shows. She was a bit too direct for my liking. Her inexperience was very much in evidence, I'm afraid," Bolger said.

"Well, never mind. At least you got the fingerprints," Lyons said, hoping that Bolger would give Mary the credit for that at least, but he said nothing.

When they arrived at the airport, Charlie Willis, the manager from the flying club, and Fergal O'Dwyer, the IAA inspector, were supervising the unloading of the broken aeroplane from the low-loader in the hangar. Some sort of yellow mini crane had been arranged, and the Cessna was suspended in broad canvas straps as they inched it up, clear of the trailer, and swung it gently around, lowering it onto the floor where canvas sheets had been laid out to receive it. All the loose bits were removed from the lorry that had brought the plane in, and placed alongside the fuselage on the canvas sheets.

As they stood and watched the unloading, a third man came into the hangar and walked across to Willis.

"Jesus, Charlie, what a mess," the man said.

Willis introduced the new arrival as Terry Normoyle. Normoyle was a skinny man in his sixties, with thinning grey hair and a rather stooped posture, probably caused by his constant bending over engines as he had worked on them over the years.

"Ah, Mr Normoyle," Lyons said, "I wonder if we could have a word in the office?" Lyons asked. Bolger made no move to go with the two of them, and Lyons was quite happy with that arrangement.

Lyons sat down with Terry Normoyle in the portacabin.

"I understand you were the last person to do work on Alpha Tango, Mr Normoyle?" Lyons said.

"Well, not quite the last, Inspector. I never fitted that bit of plastic rubbish to the engine, that's for sure," Normoyle said.

"So, how do you think it got there then?"

"Search me. We only use certified parts here. You can see from the maintenance records. I haven't seen the tubing that you recovered from the plane, but Charlie tells me it was just some clear plastic shit," Normoyle said.

"Yes, that's correct. Do you have any of that kind of material here at all, for any other purpose?" Lyons said.

"No, not that I know of anyway. You might find some of it over at the old terminal building. They had a bar over there at one time. It could have been used for the beer or something, I don't know," Normoyle said.

"Does anyone from the club have access to the old terminal?"

"No, I don't think so. It's all locked up now since the scheduled flights stopped."

"Mr Normoyle, may I ask you if you ever make home brew at home, or wine, or anything like that?" Lyons asked.

"What? No, I don't – oh, I see where you're coming from."

Normoyle leaned forward in his seat, and fixed Lyons earnestly with a stare as he spoke.

"Look Inspector, let's be very clear here. I have not ever had anything whatever to do with clear plastic tubing. I have never ever installed anything like that into an aircraft's engine, and I never will. What's more, I love aeroplanes. If that sounds daft, I've been working on them for over forty years, and I would never do anything that might compromise the safety of a plane – ever. So, I'm afraid you're barking up the wrong tree if you think I had anything to do with this terrible tragedy," Normoyle said.

"OK, I understand, thanks, Mr Normoyle. Any thoughts on anyone who might have had something to do with it?" Lyons said, thinking it was worth a try in any case.

"None. Mr Fortune has done a lot for this club. He's well liked here, and I don't know anyone who would want to do him harm. He'll be sorely missed."

"One final thing, Mr Normoyle, I'll need to get your fingerprints for the purpose of elimination," Lyons said.

"That's no problem."

Lyons took the neat little electronic fingerprint machine out of her bag and Normoyle obliged.

The two of them strolled back across the apron of the airport to the hangar where the Cessna had now been completely unloaded. Lyons beckoned Bolger across to the door, out of earshot of the others.

"James, get over to the old bar at the far side of the apron. Have a snoop around inside – see if there's any plastic tubing kicking around, you know, like attached to the old beer coolers or anything. Or if there's any evidence of any having been removed recently," she said.

Bolger ambled off in the direction of the old terminal building.

"Will you be much longer here, Mr O'Dwyer?" she asked the IAA man.

"This is where my work really begins, Inspector. I need to label all the loose bits, and examine everything very carefully. I'll need to write it all up too – we have to produce very detailed reports on every one of these accidents. It helps the manufacturers improve the safety of their machines, and especially where there has been loss of life, they will be looking to be exonerated," O'Dwyer said.

"I see. Well, I'd better leave you to get on with it then. I'd appreciate it if you could let me know if you find anything else of interest," Lyons said, handing the man her business card.

Lyons walked out of the hangar, and met James Bolger coming back across the apron.

"Well?" she said.

"Nothing, boss. It's all locked up. I couldn't get in."

"For heaven's sake, James! Could you not just use your loaf and get inside – it's hardly Fort bloody Knox!" Lyons said.

"Go back to the car, and wait for me there," she barked.

Bolger slinked off, feeling quite miserable. Did she really expect him to actually break in to the terminal building?

Lyons circled around the old deserted terminal till she found a window that had been boarded up; the plywood was rotting at the bottom corner. She pulled at it, and it gave way easily, allowing her to scramble up onto the sill and climb inside.

The old place was damp and musty, with discarded papers, empty bottles and other debris strewn around. She figured she wasn't the first person to break in. She found the bar in the half light – there was no electricity connected, so she used the torch in her phone to help her to see what she was doing.

Behind the bar she found the beer coolers, covered in dust and grime and beginning to rust. She pulled at them, but found them still attached with thick plastic piping to the taps that had once dispensed cool pints of beer to thirsty travellers. All the pipes were intact.

Chapter Thirteen

Derek Williams, Emma Fortune's form teacher, had arranged to come in to Mill Street to meet Detective Eamon Flynn at ten o'clock. Flynn showed him to the most comfortable of the station's interview rooms, and asked if he would like tea or coffee. Williams opted for a coffee, and Flynn came back a few minutes later with drinks for them both.

"Thanks for coming in, Mr Williams. This is a very sad business. I won't keep you long. We're talking to anyone who has connections to the family, just to be thorough," Flynn said.

"Of course, that's no problem. How can I help?"

"Well, just how well did you know Emma? Have you ever met her parents, that sort of thing?" Flynn asked.

"I know – sorry knew – Emma pretty well. She was a bright student, and was also fairly heavily involved in sports. I help out with the girls' hockey team as well, and Emma was a bit of a star on the hockey pitch," Williams said.

"I see. So, was she popular then?"

"Oh yes, very. She had lots of friends at the school. She hung around with a group of about five other girls in particular."

"Was there any one of the five that she was particularly close to?" Flynn said.

"Well, I can't be completely sure, but I'd say Amy Cunningham was probably her best friend – her 'bestie' as they call them these days. They were always in each other's company."

"Do you have an address for the Cunningham girl?" Flynn said.

"Not on me, but I can get it from the school of course. Why do you need to speak to her?" Williams said.

"Ah, you know how it is. We have to cross all the t's and dot all the i's in these cases. Three people died after all."

"Yes, I know, but you can't think it was anything to do with Emma, surely?"

"No, of course not. What do you know about her father?" Flynn said.

"Just that he was a big noise in the building trade. But he was good to the school. He helped us with some building work at a very reasonable price. And those portacabins we put in last year are his. They're on loan till we get proper buildings put up," Williams said.

"Did Emma ever have any trouble in school, Mr Williams?"

"Trouble. What sort of trouble?" Williams said.

"Oh, you know how teenage girls can be sometimes. Was she ever bullied, or picked upon by anyone? Maybe some of the other girls were jealous of her, that sort of thing." Flynn said.

"No, there was nothing like that. You have to understand, Emma was a very nice girl. She had a genuinely lovely personality. She'll be sorely missed in the school," Williams said, and looked down at the floor. Flynn thought that he saw the start of a tear in the man's eyes.

"OK. Well, thanks again for coming in, Mr Williams. We'll leave it at that for now. If you could just get me Amy Cunningham's details and phone them through, that would be very helpful," Flynn said, standing up and giving the man a card.

"Yes. Yes, of course," the teacher said, regaining his composure.

* * *

It was late afternoon by the time Lyons brought the team back together to discover what had been revealed about the victims of the crash.

Flynn filled them in on his discussion with Emma Fortune's form teacher. Then Lyons asked Sally Fahy what she had discovered about Barbara Fortune.

"Quite a bit actually, boss. Firstly, it looks as if she was about to get a divorce from her husband," Fahy said.

"Wow, how the hell did you get that little nugget of information?" Lyons asked.

"A very chatty daily help. Margaret Guilfoyle by name. I rang the house to see if Mrs Fortune had returned from Dublin, and she answered the phone, so I dropped out to see her. As we sat, drank several cups of tea and ate delicious homemade rock buns, Mrs Guilfoyle told me the whole story."

"Well, don't keep us in suspense then, what did she say?" Lyons said.

"It seems Barbara Fortune has been having an affair with a solicitor from Dublin for some time. And Ger Fortune knew about it too. Guilfoyle said that she witnessed several heated arguments between the two of them in the house when she was cleaning the place. Pretty nasty stuff, she said," Fahy reported.

"Did Mrs Guilfoyle say that there were any threats made by either of them against the other?" Lyons asked.

"No, not directly, but she did say that Mr Fortune had threatened his wife with never seeing their daughter again if she left him, and Mrs Fortune had replied to the effect that she didn't care about that, 'she's not even my daughter, anyway' she had said."

"I see. What did you make of that remark?" Eamon Flynn asked Fahy.

"When I got back to the office, I did some more digging. It turns out Ger Fortune was married before, and Emma was his child from his previous marriage. His first wife died tragically in a car crash when Emma was only five, and he went on to marry Barbara a few years later. She had been his secretary in his building firm it seems. I got all that from the local paper. It was quite big news at the time," Fahy said.

"Crikey, well done you, Sally," Lyons said. "And of course, that does sort of give us a motive, in a way."

"How do you mean, boss?" Bolger asked.

"Well, if Barbara Fortune was going to divorce her husband, presumably she would only get a portion of his accumulated wealth as a settlement, and maybe not a very big portion if it turned out that she was the cause of the split. Whereas now, I presume she'll inherit the lot. Tomorrow, Sally, I want you to see what Ger Fortune's estate runs to, if you can. Are there are any big insurance policies? And have a look at whatever he has tied up in the company. Meantime, James, I think someone had better have a chat with the grieving widow, don't you?" Lyons said.

"Yes, boss. Good idea," Bolger said.

"Liam, what did you get from Fortune's office?" Lyons said.

"Quite a bit, but I haven't had a chance to go through it yet. I got Ger Fortune's laptop; it was in his office, and I got the diaries like you asked – they go back a good few years, so it will take me a good bit of time to go through them, even with Mary's help," the young Garda said.

"OK. Well, give the computer to John and let him at it, see if he can find anything of interest," Lyons said.

"What exactly are we looking for?" Bolger said.

"Anything that could give us a clue as to who disliked Ger Fortune enough to sabotage his aircraft. Correspondence, emails, that sort of thing."

"Oh, right, I see what you mean," Bolger said.

"Right, well that's enough to be getting on with. Sally, will you contact Barbara Fortune and make an appointment for her to come into the station some time tomorrow for a chat? Don't be too heavy handed with her – we don't want her to take off – but make it clear we're serious all the same," Lyons said.

"James, I want you to help Liam go through the paperwork from Fortune's office. And while you're at it, why don't you arrange to drop in on his current secretary at his office tomorrow and see if there's anything she can tell you?" she continued.

* * *

When Lyons got back to her office, she put a call in to Mick Hays.

"Hi, how's it going?" she said.

"Ah, you know. More bloody spreadsheets. Oh, by the way, I have to go to a thing in town later on. Some gig the mayor is hosting. I won't be late, but I'll have to put in an appearance for an hour or so," Hays said.

"Ooh, does that mean you will have to dress up in your sexy Superintendent's uniform with a crisp, starched white shirt? I really fancy you in that outfit, you know," she said softly into the phone.

"Behave, Maureen. But don't wait for me for dinner. See you later!"

"See ya!"

When Lyons had finished talking to Hays, she decided she would go back out to the airport and have a snoop around. She had found in the past that being close to a crime scene had helped her to figure out what had actually happened, and that broken plane was the nearest she was going to get. Besides, with Mick out for the evening, there was nothing to rush home for.

She drove out through the evening traffic, and turned into the airport compound. The hangar door was pulled tight across the front of the space where the plane was being stored. Lyons parked up and got out of the car. There was no one in the portacabin used by Charlie Willis. Neither was there any sign of Normoyle or O'Dwyer – they must have all gone home for the night.

Lyons walked across to the hangar and tried the large concertina door at the front, but she couldn't budge it. She walked around the building, down along the side through the grass that was growing up against it, and turned the corner to take her along the back. She found a small door at the rear of the building that didn't appear to be locked, but it was very stiff, having fallen down slightly off its hinges through disrepair. Lyons heaved at it, and managed to get it open just wide enough to slip in sideways into the hangar.

Inside, the place was in half darkness, the only light coming in through a few sheets of what had once been clear Perspex set into the roof. The broken Cessna took up most of the available space. Parts had been removed, and were laid out in neat rows along the ground beneath the plane's one good wing. Lyons noticed that labels had been attached to identify each part. There was a very strong smell of fuel in the hangar. She hadn't remembered the smell being so strong the first time she was there, but reckoned that the fact that the place was all closed up probably accounted for it.

She edged her way along the side of the fuselage, making for the open door near the front of the plane. She wanted to look inside. As she reached the door of the plane, she leant into the cockpit to look at the floor and search in the narrow gaps between the seats. Behind her, she heard a whooshing sound, and as she turned to see what was causing it, a lick of blue flame shot across the canvas towards her. Lyons turned to go back the way she had come, but there were now flames spreading quickly all over the canvas that the plane was resting on. The plane's tyres had started to burn too, and there was acrid black smoke beginning to fill the space.

Lyons had, at one time, dated a fireman from Galway, and she remembered him telling her that if she was ever caught in a fire, in a house for example, to get down low and get out fast. She got down on all fours and tried to see through the increasing smokescreen where the door was that she had come in by. The fire had really taken hold by now, and the flames were consuming the available oxygen in the enclosed space, making breathing difficult. She started coughing, the fumes from the plastic parts, now well ablaze, catching the back of her throat. Her eyes were streaming, making it impossible to see anything at all. She had to try and get out by feel alone. Lyons knew that she had to make it out of the building, otherwise she would be burnt alive. She dropped to her belly and crawled further back, wriggling along in the dirt. She thought she could see a crack of light that must have been coming in through the back door of the building. She wriggled on, desperate to get away from the advancing flames.

She managed to get to the door and squeeze herself out into the open air. But she wasn't out of danger yet. The hangar was now fully ablaze, and large bits of debris, some of it still burning, crashed down around her as she lay on the grass struggling for breath. She staggered away and finally got to the safety of the concrete apron, where she sat down, coughing and gasping, her hands, face and clothes black with soot from the fire.

When she had recovered sufficiently to speak coherently, she reached into her jacket pocket and pulled out her phone. She called the fire brigade first and summoned them to the airport. Then she called Mill

Street, and asked Sergeant Flannery to get in touch with Detective Inspector Bolger and Detective Sergeant Sally Fahy and get them out to the airport. Only then did she relax sufficiently to realise just how close to death she had come.

Chapter Fourteen

It took the fire brigade, who had deployed four appliances to the scene, almost two hours to extinguish the blaze at the airport. There was very little left of the hangar, apart from the four walls, now blackened and cracked from the heat of the fire. The roof was all but gone, with just a few arcs of twisted steel reaching up towards the evening sky like the ribs of some dismembered animal lying on its back.

Bolger and Fahy had arrived at the scene soon after Lyons had called them, and Bolger had gone off and found some hot coffee which he gave to Lyons who was sitting sideways on the passenger seat in the doorway of her own car, shivering, more from shock than cold. Several uniformed Gardaí were also in attendance, but there was little they could do, other than secure what was left of the building.

"You'd better get Sinéad Loughran out here too," Lyons said to Fahy, "there may be some forensics to be found, although I doubt it to be honest."

"Do you think someone knew you were inside?" Bolger asked.

"Who knows. It was clearly more of an effort to destroy evidence than murder a Garda, wouldn't you say?"

"Yes, probably. But still, it escalates matters somewhat, doesn't it?" Bolger said.

"It certainly does that, Inspector, it certainly does."

* * *

Lyons arrived home just as Hays was parking his car in the drive of their house in Salthill. When he saw his partner, her face still blackened from the smoke, he couldn't believe his eyes.

Inside the house, Lyons explained the events of the evening to Hays.

"Bet you didn't have as much excitement with the Mayor?" she said, pouring them both a stiff brandy.

"God, Maureen, it's no laughing matter. You could have been killed," he said, "anyway – who says I didn't?"

"Go on."

"Well, our old friend James McMahon was at the do. He gave me what may turn out to be some useful information, as it happens," Hays said.

"Not just the name of some tasty Eastern European tart then?" she said.

"Now, now. Don't be like that. He's changed his ways since then. No, he said we should have a look at a Tony Fallon. Apparently when the crash came, Fortune left him badly stuck. He used to run a company called Fallon's Floors and Doors. McMahon used him for some of the fancier houses he was building during the Celtic Tiger. But it went bust in 2010, largely thanks to our Mr Fortune, it seems. Anyway, that's not what matters for now. Thank heavens you're OK," Hays said.

"Ah, look on the bright side, Mick, it would have saved you the cost of a cremation if I hadn't managed to get out!"

"Come here," he said, drawing Lyons close.

"Jesus, you smell awful! Your hair is full of smoke," he said, turning Lyons' face up to his and kissing her slowly on the mouth.

"Now, go and have a bath," Hays said.

"Only if you come and scrub my back, Superintendent," Lyons said, pulling him along by his tie.

* * *

The following morning Hays and Lyons arrived in Mill Street together. Hays accompanied her as she assembled the entire team.

"What about your precious spreadsheets?" Lyons asked him as they went into the overflow building just down the road from the Garda Station.

"They can bloody well wait. There must be some advantages to being a senior officer," Hays said.

Fahy and Bolger had stayed with the fire brigade till well into the evening, and they remained with the forensic team at the airport too, as they went about trying to find evidence of the cause of the fire.

Despite their late shift, all of the team were present in the briefing room, and they each asked after Lyons in turn when she came in. They were surprised at how well she looked after her ordeal, although inside, she felt quite badly shaken up.

"Now, you're all aware of what took place last night out at the flying club. It looks like it was a deliberate attempt to destroy evidence, although to be honest, we had already removed the offending part from the plane long before it was left in the hangar. But it's clear, someone felt the necessity to burn the place down just in case. But that's not all. Superintendent Hays has received information about a Tony Fallon as well that we need to follow up. So, who can make some room in their busy day today to sort that out?" Lyons said.

Liam Walsh put up his hand.

"I can make some time, boss. What do you want me to do?"

"See if you can find out where he is these days. He had a showroom and workshop on the industrial estate round by Sandy Row. Go and have a look – see if anyone remembers him, or knows where he is now," Lyons said.

"And James, when you're going through the paperwork from Fortune's office, keep an eye out for the name Fallon, or Floors and Doors. There might be something," she said.

"Sally, did you get in touch with Barbara Fortune?" Lyons asked.

"Yes, sorry, what with all the fuss out at the airport, I'd forgotten all about her. She's coming in later, boss," Fahy said.

"Good. Remember now, she has a motive for the death of her husband, and she didn't seem to be too bothered about the daughter either when we broke the news to her, so better take James along. Oh, and find out from her if Fortune was insured too," Lyons said.

"What about Devaney? Has anyone followed up on him? We've all been totally focused on Fortune, but we mustn't overlook the fact that three people died in this thing. Mary, can you do some more digging on Devaney? And listen, folks, we need to pick up the pace on this a bit. It's been a few days now, and we don't seem to be any further on yet," Lyons said.

Just as Lyons was bringing the briefing to an end, a uniformed Garda from the main station appeared in the doorway.

"Sorry to disturb you, Inspector, but there's a Mr O'Dwyer from the Irish Aviation Authority asking for you at the front desk."

"Thanks, Padraig, I'll be along directly. Show him into the better interview room and see if he wants a cup of tea, will you?" Lyons said.

* * *

Lyons joined Fergal O'Dwyer in the small, but newly painted interview room, bringing her own cup of coffee in with her.

"Good morning, Mr O'Dwyer. Thanks for coming in. I suppose you've heard about the goings on out at the airport last night?" Lyons said, taking a seat in front of the low coffee table that had replaced the previous one that had been bolted to the floor.

"Yes, indeed. That must have been very frightening for you. Are you OK?" he said.

"It certainly was. But I'm OK, thanks. I'm made of pretty tough stuff," she said.

O'Dwyer decided not to comment, though he was sure she was right in her self-assessment.

"Any sign of whoever it was that started the fire?"

"No, none. He, or perhaps she, must have been there at the same time as I was, and when they saw me going into the hangar they must have decided to kill two birds with one stone, as it were. Our forensic team found a trail of fuel leading from a grassy patch to the left of the hangar, in under the door. So that's where the fire was started from," Lyons said.

"Anything else of interest? Footprints? Tyre tracks, that sort of thing?" O'Dwyer said.

"Maybe, but the fire department will have obliterated anything useful tramping all over the place in their big boots."

"Look, I know this may sound a bit odd, but the fire has left the IAA with a dilemma. I've been speaking to my boss back in Dublin, and he's very concerned about the destruction of any evidence linked to the accident. These small planes don't have black boxes, but we can often re-construct the final minutes of flight from the instruments, and Alpha Tango was pretty well equipped in that regard. All the latest stuff. But now that it's been destroyed, well that's that," O'Dwyer said.

"So, what's the dilemma?" Lyons said.

"It's been suggested that we do a reconstruction. You know, take one of the other Cessnas up, follow the same route, and see what happens when we switch off the engine. I need to get some measurements under the same circumstances as the accident just to make sure that there was nothing else going on."

"Isn't that a bit reckless?" Lyons said.

"No, not really. I'd be at the controls. I'm about the same height and weight as Ger Fortune, and I can assure you if it came to it, I have landed many an aircraft with the engine out over the years. But that won't arise in any case – all we need to do is restart it before it gets too low and slow."

"Hmmm, I see. And who else would be with you?" Lyons asked, but she already knew what was coming next.

"Well that's just it. We need two more passengers that are the same weight and height as Devaney and Emma. I was hoping to persuade Charlie Willis to play the part of Devaney," O'Dwyer said.

"And what about someone for Emma?"

"That's where we have an issue. Sandra is too tall and a good bit heavier than Emma was, and I don't mean that in an unkind way. But we have to get as close to the actual event as possible, and payload is an important factor in the sink rate of the plane once the engine has cut out. You see the thing is, Inspector, you're just about a dead ringer for Emma as far as stature and build is concerned." O'Dwyer had the good sense to say nothing more.

Lyons digested his suggestion. Not content to have her roasted alive, they now wanted to put her into a lethal aeroplane crash as well, just to finish the job off. Well, she was damned if she was going to let this get the better of her!

"Well it is a bit unorthodox, Mr O'Dwyer, but if it will help you to determine the exact cause of the crash, then I suppose we could give it a go. But I should warn you, killing off Garda Inspectors doesn't go down very well in these parts, so you had better be the ace aviator you say you are," Lyons said, and fixed him with an earnest stare.

Again, O'Dwyer remained silent.

"When do you want to do this?" she asked a moment later.

"I was thinking tomorrow. The forecast is just about the same as the day of the accident, and visibility should be similar too. Now we won't be going out over the sea this time, I have worked out a flight plan that will simulate Alpha Tango's trip without doing that. And don't worry, Inspector, you'll be perfectly safe. Trust me," he said.

"Of course, what could possibly go wrong?" she said ironically.

"But I want this done by the book. I want a letter of authorisation from the IAA, and I'll get one from Superintendent Hays too. You'll need to indemnify all the civilians involved as well. Can you see to that?" Lyons said.

"Yes, Inspector, all in hand."

"And what exactly are you hoping to achieve with this daredevil stunt, Mr O'Dwyer?" Lyons asked, having some second thoughts about the whole caper.

"Once I switch off the engine, I will have some extra gear connected up to the plane to monitor and measure various metrics. The time and distance to the ground will tell us how the pilot reacted to the emergency, and if he followed normal 'dead stick' procedures. I'll be straight with you, Inspector. There are some in head office who have suggested that Ger Fortune's actions may have been deliberate," O'Dwyer said.

"What? Suicide?"

"Exactly. It happens, you know. Not very often, thank heavens, but it does happen, and the strange thing is that it is perfectly straightforward to land a Cessna 172 with a dead engine if you know what you're doing, as you will see tomorrow. So, the question remains," O'Dwyer said.

Chapter Fifteen

Liam Walsh brought the squad car to a halt outside the unit that was designated number eight on Boolavogue Road, part of the Sandy Row business complex. He had come alone, as all the other members of the detective team were engaged on other tasks, so he was acutely aware that his performance on this particular mission would be critically appraised by Inspector Lyons.

Walsh was a young detective Garda, but he was ambitious. He was keen to make detective sergeant as soon as possible, mostly to get a better pay grade, so that he could get a mortgage on a house. He was dating a pretty nurse from the regional hospital, and he wanted to propose to her before some other Lothario with deeper pockets stepped in and snatched her away from him. He also knew that although Eamon Flynn had been passed over for promotion to inspector in the recent re-shuffle, it wouldn't be long before that appointment was made, leaving a gap at sergeant level for him to fill. If only they could get rid of that fool Bolger!

Number eight was now a busy coffee shop with a sign over the door announcing 'Kool Koffee – *the coolest place for a hot drink.*' The shop front was painted a dull but fashionable grey colour, and inside the floor was bare boards, adding to the din being made by the patrons as well as the inevitable hiss and gurgle of the coffee machine itself. Walsh asked for the manager, and after a moment or two waiting at the cash register, a tall dark-haired girl with a long ponytail and a tag bearing the name 'Klara' appeared.

Walsh asked Klara if she had any knowledge of the previous owner of the unit, explaining that it had been a showroom for wooden floors and doors.

"No, I'm sorry. I am only here a few months. But maybe you could try the hardware shop two doors down. I think he has been here a long time," Klara said.

Walsh left, feeling a bit hard done by that he hadn't been offered a coffee.

The shop two doors down was one of those country hardware shops that sells absolutely everything, most of which was on display both outside and inside the premises. With so much stock, there was hardly any room inside, but Walsh found a man, clearly in his sixties, wearing a brown shop coat standing behind a small clear area of counter space that also accommodated a cash register.

"Can I help you?" the man said as Walsh entered the shop.

"Hi. I am Detective Garda Walsh from Mill Street. I'm trying to find out about a man who ran the place two doors down before the coffee shop took over," Walsh said, indicating the direction with his hand.

"Ah, Tony. Yes, I remember him OK. Floors and Doors, he called it. He did well there too, until the crash came. Nice fella. He always seemed cheerful, except at the end, of course, when he had to close the business. He'd been there a good few years by then. Not as long as me, but he was no blow-in," the man said, apparently reminiscing fondly about what he undoubtedly saw as better times.

"Yes, that's him. What was his surname, do you recall?"

"Fallon, Tony Fallon, that was it. He had his name over the door," the man confirmed.

"Any idea where he is now, Mr eh …?" Walsh said.

"Byrne, Tommy Byrne, that's me. Now, let me see, the last I heard of Tony Fallon he was working with the forestry up at Terryland, out on the Headford Road. But I don't know if he's still there. Funny how you lose touch, isn't it?" Tommy said.

"Terryland, yes I think I know it. You haven't seen him in a while then?" Walsh asked.

"No, not since he closed up here. Oh wait, I did see him in O'Flaherty's Bar up the town once or twice last year, it must have been. We said hello, but that was all, he was with a bunch of mates from the job."

"OK. Thanks, Mr Byrne. That's been most helpful. I'll leave you to it then," Walsh said, and headed back to the car.

Walsh drove out to Terryland, a sprawling urban park that had been opened in 2000 by Galway Council with the ultimate aim of planting half a million trees as part of a reforestation campaign in the area.

He found the workmen's small cottage easily enough, but there was no one there, and he didn't fancy trying to locate Fallon on his own by simply walking around the park. Eventually, he left a note pinned to the door asking Tony Fallon to call Liam Walsh and giving his own mobile number.

* * *

When Lyons appeared back at the overflow unit that they were housed in, Inspector James Bolger asked for a word in private.

They went to Lyons' office.

"What's on your mind, James?"

"Look, Inspector, I'm not happy being asked to go through piles of paper and computer records here in the station, when there's a triple murder to be solved. I'm not a bloody pen pusher, you know?" he said, his normally calm face reddening somewhat as he spoke.

"I see. So, what is it that you think you ought to be doing then, James?"

"I don't know. I need to be out there – detecting, not shuffling paper with some rookie here in the station. That's not what inspectors do."

Lyons was loving it. She was going to enjoy the outcome of this discussion greatly, and she wondered just how much rope Bolger would need before he hanged himself.

"You're right, of course, James. I'm sure you'd much rather be locked into a burning aircraft hangar with the flames licking up around your man bits, or maybe struggling through three feet of bog water in your waders looking for evidence in the rain. Is that more what you had in mind?" she said.

"No, of course not. But there must be something meaningful I can do. I'm going stir crazy here."

"Tell you what, James. Why don't you go right back to your pile of old papers and keep digging for a while, and I'll see if I can think up something more suitable for an action man that you can do this afternoon. How's that?"

"Great. Thanks, boss. Talk later." He left the room feeling reassured.

"God, give me strength," she said to herself, shaking her head, when he had gone. Then an idea struck her.

She called Fergal O'Dwyer on his mobile.

When she had finished the call, she went and found Inspector James Bolger.

"James. I have just the thing. Tomorrow morning, I want you out with me to the airport. We have a little job to do that will take an hour or two. OK?"

"Yes, thanks, boss. Nice one."

"Oh, and James, I suggest you wear your brown trousers," Lyons said.

Bolger looked perplexed, but said nothing, and went back to shuffling through the contents of Ger Fortune's office.

Chapter Sixteen

The following morning, just as O'Dwyer had predicted, was largely clear, with only a few small clouds high up in the sky passing slowly out to the east.

"So, what's this job then, boss?" Bolger asked Lyons as they drove out towards the airport in Lyons' car.

"All in good time, James. You'll see. But it's not pushing paper, that's for sure."

When they arrived at the airport, they made their way into the flying club portacabin, where Willis, Normoyle and O'Dwyer were already assembled, poring over an Ordnance Survey map of West Galway.

"Ah, Inspectors, come in. We're just going over the route here. Fergal has mapped out a trip that's about the same distance as the Fortunes took, but it doesn't involve any over water flying," Charlie Willis said.

"Good," Lyons said, and turning to Terry Normoyle, she asked, "and is the plane we're going to use in top class order?"

"Yes, of course, it's Yankee Zulu which is a sister ship to Alpha Tango." Normoyle said, looking a little forlornly out of the window to where another Cessna 172 stood gleaming in the bright sunshine.

"And is all the paperwork in order now, Fergal?" Lyons said.

"Yes, yes it is. I have the indemnities you asked for, and I've left a copy of my PPL and log book with Charlie here. He's going to man the radio, and we'll be in touch constantly," he replied.

"Right then, if we're ready. Let's go," O'Dwyer said.

James Bolger took Lyons aside as they left the portacabin.

"What's going on, boss. What are we doing?" he said.

"We're going to take part in a reconstruction of the accident so that we can find out exactly what happened. We're going up in the plane, James, and when we have been flying around for about an hour, the engine will cut out, and Fergal O'Dwyer is going to take measurements from the instrumentation," Lyons said, deadpan.

"You've got to be joking! I'm not getting up in that thing! That's suicide," Bolger stuttered.

"Now, look here, Inspector Bolger. You wanted some adventure – I'm giving you adventure. Now stop being such a bloody wuss and let's get on with it. You're making a show of us. And anyway, if it all goes belly up, the death in service benefit in the Garda pension scheme is quite generous!" she said.

She turned away, as she couldn't help smiling to herself.

* * *

Lyons sat in the back seat of the Cessna just as Emma Fortune had done on the ill-fated flight. Bolger got into the right-hand seat in front, and Fergal O'Dwyer did the walk-around checks, making sure that the control surfaces were free and there were no loose bits hanging off the plane.

When O'Dwyer climbed in, he put on his headphones and called Charlie Willis on the radio.

"Clear to start and taxi to the threshold of runway two-six Fergal," Willis said.

"Start and taxi to two-six," O'Dwyer repeated.

The Cessna set off, making the short bumpy journey across the apron to the start of the runway, and lined up.

"Yankee Zulu, cleared take off runway two-six – wind two-ninety at five," Willis' voice said in their headsets.

"Cleared take off, runway two-six, rolling, roger," O'Dwyer repeated.

O'Dwyer advanced the throttle, and the little plane lurched forward before settling down into a rapidly accelerating run along the tarmac. O'Dwyer eased back on the yoke, and the Cessna lifted obediently into the air, drifting slightly sideways against the wind.

Their route took them out past the city, over Moycullen, and then on towards Inverin, where O'Dwyer would start his experiment. With a bit of luck, when the engine cut out, even if he couldn't get it started again, O'Dwyer could navigate to the runway at Inverin and land there, although he had several other options lined up in case that was not possible.

The Connemara bogland looked stunning in the morning sunlight, and they got a good view of the Twelve Pins off in the distance, looking every bit as blue as they did in a Paul Henry painting. The flight was largely smooth, though occasionally the little plane bumped along in response to a thermal current coming up off the warming land beneath, or a gust, as a cloud passed overhead.

O'Dwyer kept in touch with the flying club as they flew along, and as they neared the target area, he switched to Inverin tower, where the controllers had been fully briefed about the peculiarities of this specific flight.

They had been flying for almost an hour, and even James Bolger appeared to be settling down in the cramped quarters of the Cessna's cabin.

"Right, here goes," O'Dwyer said, and reached forward to turn the key on the dashboard to the "Off" position. The engine of the plane cut out immediately, and an eerie silence descended on them. The prop stopped turning, and the nose of the little plane fell away towards the ground.

O'Dwyer was on the radio immediately. "Inverin tower, this is Yankee Zulu, dead stick approximately two miles east of the field. Request immediate clearance to land," he said calmly into his microphone.

"Roger, Yankee Zulu, cleared to land runway two-three, wind two-eight-zero at four knots, gusting to ten. Do you require assistance on landing?" the controller said.

"Negative, Inverin. Will advise further when landed," O'Dwyer said.

"Aren't you going to restart the engine?" Bolger said nervously.

"Only if I have to for safety reasons. I need to collect data all the way down to the ground if possible, but if it becomes dangerous, then I'll get the engine going again. Don't worry," O'Dwyer said.

The Cessna 172 has an incredibly slow stall speed. Even fully laden, with flaps extended, the plane will still fly at forty knots, which makes it relatively easy to land without power. The key to success is to watch the airspeed like a hawk. Many pilots will try to keep the nose level by pulling back on the yoke. This feels better, but it's all too easy to let the speed decay to dangerous levels by doing this, and inducing a stall. At low altitude, it is hard to recover, and it usually ends in disaster. O'Dwyer let the nose dip to maintain speed, and said to Bolger, who was now looking decidedly green beside him, "Keep your eyes fixed on this dial here – it's the airspeed indicator. If it goes below fifty – shout, and don't hang about."

With an altitude of just under 1500 feet, and with two miles to go to the runway at Inverin, O'Dwyer calculated that they were easily within striking distance of the airport. Inside the small craft, Bolger was transfixed on the air speed indicator, willing it to stay above fifty, and Lyons was quite relaxed in the rear of the aircraft, keeping quiet, so as not to distract Fergal O'Dwyer from his delicate task.

As the plane descended, O'Dwyer gently nudged it around to the runway heading, and it wasn't long before they could see the concrete strip dead ahead. The airport has no landing aids, so the approach was purely visual, and O'Dwyer seemed to be making a good job of it. But as the plane got closer to the ground, some buffeting occurred, causing James Bolger to emit a high-pitched squeal, and O'Dwyer to jerk the yoke around a bit to steady the approach. Inside the aircraft, the tension was palpable, and everyone seemed to be holding their breath.

A minute or so later, the Cessna's wheels touched down, and O'Dwyer was able to use the residual momentum in the plane to steer it off the runway onto one of the taxiways. As it came to a halt, all three let out a collective sigh of relief, and Lyons said, "Well done Fergal, that was exhilarating, thanks."

"Told ye it would be fine," O'Dwyer said cheerfully.

Bolger opened the side door of the aircraft, stumbled out, and proceeded to vomit into the grass. When he straightened up, his face was whiter than the paint on the side of the plane.

"Never mind, James," Lyons said, joining him on the taxiway, "just the return journey to look forward to now!"

"Why don't you two go into the building and get a cup of tea. I'll follow you in shortly, I need to record the readings from the instrumentation that I fitted yesterday," O'Dwyer said.

"Did you get any useful data, Fergal?" Lyons said.

"I'll have to study the recordings later, but yes, I'd say I did. It's a bit early to tell, but I'd say Fortune just didn't have enough experience to land the plane safely. It's very easy to mess it up under pressure."

The Inverin traffic controller had already telephoned Charlie Willis and Terry Normoyle back in Galway to advise them that Yankee Zulu had made a safe landing, much to the considerable relief of the two men.

Bolger and Lyons headed into the coffee bar inside the terminal building and Lyons ordered two coffees and a pastry apiece.

"Here. This will settle your stomach," she said handing Bolger a plate with a shiny Danish pastry on it.

When they had seated themselves at a convenient table, Bolger said, "I'm not going back in that thing. I don't care. I'll get onto Clifden and get them to send a car for me to take me back to Galway. Do you want to come with me?"

"What, and miss out on my air miles – not likely! I take it you've had enough adventure for one day then?" she said.

"Enough for a lifetime. Anyway, how was that anything to do with our investigation?" Bolger said, still a little angry with his own performance.

"Fergal has been contacted by his head office. Someone up there put the idea in his head that it might have been suicide on the part of Ger Fortune, or that there might have been some kind of a scuffle in the cockpit when the engine cut out. He needed to collect data from a similar flight path and compare it to the information he found in Alpha Tango."

"I see. Seems a bit unlikely, but surely O'Dwyer could just have restarted the engine again before we landed," Bolger said.

"That wouldn't have been a reconstruction, it would have been a simulation," Lyons said.

"OK. Well, whatever. I'm off to get a lift organised. See you back later," Bolger said, draining his coffee and getting up from the table.

* * *

Lyons enjoyed the flight back to Galway Airport with Fergal O'Dwyer. She was warming to the man. She liked his precision and thoroughness. She felt very relaxed in his company, and she was completely confident in his now well-proven flying skills. Lyons appreciated the beautiful scenery that stretched out beneath them as they flew along at 1500 feet. The air was stiller now, having settled down from the slight turbulence they had encountered in the morning as the land had started to warm up.

When they were about half way through the thirty-minute journey, O'Dwyer asked Lyons if she would like to take the controls. He told her just to keep things steady, and showed her how to turn the plane left and right, easing back on the yoke to maintain height as the Cessna slipped into the gentle turns. He showed her how to use the throttle and the altimeter to descend to 1200 feet, and then climb again back to their cruising altitude. She loved it.

O'Dwyer took back control as they turned in over Claregalway and lined up for a straight in approach to Galway's runway two-six.

Minutes later, they were back inside the office of the flying club with Charlie Willis and Terry Normoyle.

"Where's your gentleman friend?" Normoyle said.

"Ah, we threw him out over the bog – he was getting a bit lippy," Lyons said with a perfectly straight face.

"He decided to travel back by road," corrected O'Dwyer, "he didn't much like my piloting style."

The other two looked at each other and shrugged.

"So, what now?" Lyons asked.

"I'll collate the data from the plane, then I'm just about done here. I'll write up a preliminary report later this week, and move on to the next thing," O'Dwyer said.

"And we start the tiresome business of filing an insurance claim for the loss of Alpha Tango. I don't suppose that will be an easy one," Willis said, rolling his eyes to heaven.

"That will be two claims, Charlie," said Terry Normoyle, "one for the plane and one for the hangar."

"Don't remind me, Terry. Can we call on you for evidence if we need it – for the fire I mean?" he said, turning to Lyons.

"Yes, sure, no problem. Thanks for your help everyone, I'll be off then," Lyons said, and left the airport.

* * *

Lyons got back to the station just after lunchtime, having stopped on the way for a bite to eat. She had really enjoyed the flight back with Fergal, and as she ate her sandwich at the service station and drank a strong coffee, she pondered taking a few lessons out at the flying club. She wondered what Mick would think of the idea.

"He has his beloved Folkboat, after all, and at least I'm not likely to get seasick up in the air," she rationalized to herself.

Back at the station, she met Sally Fahy in the corridor and asked her how the interview with Barbara Fortune had gone.

"She's a cool customer that one. She wanted to know how we knew about her affair in Dublin and the imminent divorce, but I didn't rat out the cleaner. She got quite flustered. But she has an alibi for the day that Fortune flew out to the islands, and the following day too," Fahy said.

"Where was she?" Lyons asked.

"Wouldn't you know – tucked up in bed in a hotel on the Naas Road with her beloved solicitor. He's married too, of course, so hence the hotel. You won't believe it, but she even had the receipt for the room in her purse. Apparently, they pay for the room turn-about, and it was her turn this time."

"Very modern, I'm sure. I must remember that when I find myself an eligible solicitor to have an affair with – NOT!" Lyons said.

Fahy laughed. The Gardaí in general didn't like solicitors much, and Lyons in particular had had some very difficult experiences with them. She remembered the slimy individual they had to deal with when they arrested Ciaran O'Shaughnessy for the murder of his uncle out at Derrygimlagh a few years back.

"And you're happy with the woman's alibi, are you?" Lyons said.

"It looks sound enough, boss, and she doesn't look like the type of person to go messing around with bits of plastic tubing either. I don't think she's our murderer," Fahy said.

"Pity. Well, thanks anyway. Have you written it up in the system yet?" Lyons asked.

"Just on my way to do it now. How did your adventure go, and what have you done with the boy wonder?" Fahy asked.

Lyons laughed at the reference.

"Ah, don't, will ye. We scared the shite out of him in the plane, and he's sulking his way back by car. Should be here by about four," Lyons said.

"Jeez, Maureen, you're wicked. What will you tell the Super?"

"Fuck it, Sally, he's an idiot. Not Mick – Bolger. He'll need to sort himself out pretty bloody smartly unless he wants to spend a few weeks on car park duty down at the cattle market," Lyons said.

"I've heard a few stories, OK. But don't worry, what goes around comes around," Fahy said, and set off down the corridor towards the evidence room.

* * *

Lyons was busy updating the Garda PULSE system with the new information that they had gathered as a result of the reconstruction, when Inspector Bolger eventually appeared back in the office.

"You made it then, boss," he said to Lyons with a sheepish grin on his face.

"Apparently. And a darn sight quicker than you did too, by the looks of it. And I have a note to call Séan Mulholland out in Clifden. I hope you didn't cause any trouble out there?"

"What, me – never! Oh, by the way, I came across that geezer you were asking about in some of Fortune's papers before I was so abruptly removed from that task. Fallon, Tony Fallon it was."

"Oh. What about him?" Lyons said.

"It goes back a few years, but he wrote to Fortune looking for payment of quite a large sum of money he was owed when the crash came. Then he followed up with a solicitor's letter, and when that didn't bring a result, he wrote again. Pretty angry stuff – making threats and so on. Fortune had kept the letters in his file."

"OK. Well, dig them out and make copies. Has anyone managed to find the elusive Mr Fallon yet?" Lyons said.

"Not sure. I'll check with Liam Walsh now, and see if he's heard from him. And I think John O'Connor found something in Fortune's emails too," Bolger said.

"What sort of thing?"

"Not sure."

"Well, can you get on and pull this together this afternoon? This Fallon character could be a suspect if he's still around. And get someone to find him. You know, home address, regular haunts, that sort of thing," Lyons said, trying not to show her frustration too much.

"Where would I get his address?"

"Phone book, tax office, voters' register, driving license office, bank, credit card company, our own systems – take your pick."

"Right. I'm on the case," Bolger said and left her office.

"Idiot," Lyons said to no one in particular.

Chapter Seventeen

When Lyons got home that evening, Mick Hays was already in the house, relaxing in the sunroom overlooking the garden at the back.

"God, I've had some day," Lyons said as she flopped down on the wicker chair beside him.

"Do tell," Hays said, looking up from the papers he had balanced on his knee.

Lyons recounted the events of the day, starting with the stimulating reconstruction in the Cessna.

"I see what you mean. That must have been scary for you. If I'd known exactly what you were up to, I would probably have tried to stop you," Hays said.

"I'm glad you didn't. We could have fallen out over that," she said, taking his hand in hers and giving it a quick kiss.

"Hmm. Still, it's at times like that when my two worlds collide. I'm caught between wanting to protect the woman I love and allowing a damn fine cop with brilliant instincts to just get on with it. But I'm a bit surprised about Bolger. I thought he was made of sterner stuff."

Lyons, who was still holding Hays' hand, squeezed it gently.

"Don't get me started. To be truthful, he's becoming a bit of a laughing stock around the station. That's going to make things very difficult for him if he doesn't change his ways – and quickly," Lyons said.

"Do you think I should have a word with him?"

"It's your call, Mick, but probably, yes, before he self-destructs altogether. Even young Mary is unimpressed, and she's not exactly an old hand at this stuff."

"Right. I'll leave it for a little while till he gets over today's embarrassments, then I'll see if I can find an appropriate moment. Do you think I should say anything to Plunkett? This graduate entry malarkey was part of his grand plan after all."

"You had better forewarn him there's trouble at the mill. You might even be able to pass the buck."

"Not my style, Maureen, as you well know, but I see what you mean."

"Anyway – what's for dinner, I'm starving?" she said.

"There's a vast menu on offer from the Chinese at the corner," Hays said.

"No, let's not do that. I want a real meal. Give me ten minutes to change into some proper clothes, and then you can take me out somewhere nice. Deal?"

"Deal!"

It took Lyons more like half an hour to change her clothes and do her makeup, but it was worth it. When she reappeared, she looked radiant with her shiny dark brown hair cascading down across her shoulders, and big sparkly brown eyes. She had put on a summer dress that finished just a little above her knees, and had finished the ensemble with a pair of open-toed, high-heeled shoes.

"I am a lucky bugger," Hays said as she got to the bottom of the stairs.

"You're not that lucky, Hays. You're paying for dinner," she said with an impish smile, slipping her arm into his as they left the house.

* * *

Over a relaxed meal in the exclusive Twelve restaurant out near Bearna, they discussed the case.

"So, where are you up to with this thing, Maureen?" Hays asked when they had finished their starters of pan-fried scallops.

"The problem is, there are almost too many suspects. Fortune wasn't very popular in certain quarters, and some of the people he managed to upset aren't from the top drawer, if you know what I mean. There's quite a few that could have wished him harm."

"Yes, but there's a difference between disliking a guy, and murdering him along with his daughter and a colleague. That's fairly mainstream as far as revenge goes," Hays said.

"You're right, of course. But what other motive could there have been?"

"Have you ruled out the wife? If he was playing away – hell hath no fury, and all that."

"It looks as if she was the one that was playing away. She's having an affair with a Dublin-based solicitor. They were going to get divorced – her and Fortune I mean."

"Ouch. That could provide a motive, if she was only going to get a pittance for a divorce settlement," Hays said.

"We checked. She has a cast iron alibi. And anyway, I doubt if aircraft engines are among her core skills."

"She could have hired someone to do the deadly deed."

"That's a good point. Maybe we should have a look at her bank account, see if there are any payments or sizeable cash withdrawals unaccounted for recently," Lyons said.

"See, I'm not just a pretty face!"

"There's an answer for that, but I'm saying nothing," she said smiling. As it happened, she thought he was a fine-looking man – not exactly 'pretty', but handsome – certainly.

* * *

The following morning, Lyons was in flying form. She arrived at the office early, and as soon as Bolger appeared, she cornered him in the makeshift canteen where he was hoping to get himself a cup of coffee to start the day.

"Would you like a coffee, boss?" Bolger said.

"No time for that, James. I want you to get out and find me Mr Tony Fallon. I don't care if you have to climb every tree in that Terryland place – just bring him in. I want him sitting in front of me before lunchtime. OK?" Lyons said.

"Right, boss. I'll take Eamon and Mary with me, and we'll find him, don't worry," he said, realising that she was in no mood for procrastination or argument. He did however continue to prepare a cup of coffee for himself, but Lyons was having none of it.

"Well, what are you waiting for?" she said.

"Just on my way, boss," he said, putting down the spoon and slinking out past her to go and find the other two.

Back at her desk, Lyons followed up with Sinéad Loughran.

"Hi, Sinéad. Just wondering if there was anything significant in the post-mortems on the bodies we pulled out of the plane in the bog?"

"Hi, Maureen. No, nothing strange at all, I'm afraid. Dr Dodd did input his report into the system yesterday, I think. Did you not see it?"

"Haven't had a chance to look, Sinéad, anyway I'd rather hear it from you," Lyons said.

"Let's see. Yes, here it is. The girl, Emma, had some slight traces of weed in her system. Nothing major. Dodd said it was probably a few days old. And before you ask, we didn't find any in her baggage, so she probably has a small stash for personal use at home somewhere. Fortune had been drinking the night before the fateful flight, but it had almost all gone from his system. He certainly wasn't over the limit for flying in any case. And Devaney was completely clean. Nothing. Not even an aspirin in him," Loughran said.

"I see. Well, that's useful. Gives us a reason to go back into Fortune's house, if we need it. What sort of general health was Fortune in?"

"There's nothing noted in the file. He was a bit overweight, but everything seems to have been in working order," Loughran said.

"Did you get anything from the fire scene out at the airport?"

"Very little, Maureen. The accelerant was taken from the flying club's supply of aviation fuel, and the place had been well-doused in it. Someone was making sure there would be nothing left. The lock on the main hangar door had been forced. It wasn't very secure to begin with – just an average padlock. We found it in the grass. There were no footprints of any use, I'm afraid; we did get a thumb print off the lock, but no matches in the system," Loughran said.

"Great. Oh, just one thing, is the thumb print from a man or a woman, or can't you tell?"

"Almost certainly a man's print. Why do you ask?" Loughran said.

"Oh, nothing. Just curious."

* * *

When Lyons had finished the call with Sinéad Loughran, she went looking for John O'Connor. She found him with three PCs open on his desk, and he appeared to be working all of them pretty hard. He looked up as Lyons approached.

"Good morning, Inspector," O'Connor said.

"Morning, John. What have you here?"

"This is the daughter's laptop," he said, pointing to a neat little device with a pink plastic cover on the left of his desk. "I haven't really got into that one yet. I'm more focussed on Fortune's one."

"Anything of interest?" Lyons said.

"I'm going back over his old emails. There's only about a year's worth stored on the machine itself, but I've got into his archive now, and there's loads of stuff in there going back a good while."

"Anything nasty?"

"Well, as I was telling Inspector Bolger yesterday, there are a few choice ones from a guy called Tony Fallon who seems to have been owed a pile of cash for work carried out in 2006 and 2007. Then there are a few more from people who were owed smaller amounts, but Fallon seems to be the one who was hardest hit, and he wasn't happy about it," O'Connor said.

"Right. Well, can you print out those for me and leave them on my desk? Thanks, John. And when you get around to the girl's machine, let me know if there's anything there too, will you?"

"Yes, no problem."

Chapter Eighteen

Eamon Flynn asked Bolger to excuse him from the trip out to Terryland, saying that he needed to follow up an interview with Amy Cunningham, Emma Fortune's best friend. Bolger agreed, which left him going out to the forest park with just Mary Costelloe.

When they got to the park, Bolger told Mary to head off around the track to the east, while he would go in the other direction. She was to call him if she encountered Tony Fallon, so they could bring him in together.

Mary set off on the designated route, but after a minute or two, when she was sure Bolger was well out of the way, she doubled back and made for the cottage where the workmen had their breaks. There was no one there, but she waited around outside, and a few minutes later, a gang of five men approached the building.

"Which one of you is Tony Fallon?" she said as they approached.

"Oi, oi, Tony, what have you been up to then?" jeered two of the others, nudging one of their number on the shoulder.

"Who wants to know?" he said in response.

Fallon was a well-built man in his late forties with a head of dark hair sticking out from under a baseball cap, wearing work overalls and big heavy boots.

Costelloe held up her warrant card, and said nothing.

"What do you want?" Fallon said, the cheeriness gone from his voice.

"I'd like you to come with me to the Garda station please, Mr Fallon. We'd like to talk to you about Gerald Fortune."

"That bastard. What's he done now?" Fallon said.

"If you could just come along please, Mr Fallon, we can have a chat about it."

"OK. But I can't stay long. I need to finish my shift here, or they'll dock my pay."

Costelloe called the station on her mobile and asked for a squad car to come and collect herself and Tony Fallon to bring them back to Mill Street. The car arrived three minutes later, and they were back in the station another five minutes after that.

Costelloe phoned Lyons on the internal phone.

"I have Tony Fallon here in Interview Room Two, Inspector, if you'd like to interview him," she said.

"I thought Inspector Bolger was with you. Can't he do it?"

"He's still out at Terryland, Inspector. I kind of lost him out there," Costelloe said.

"Terrific! OK. I'll be down directly. Get him a cuppa, will you, and settle him in?"

* * *

"Good morning, Mr Fallon, my name is Senior Inspector Lyons. Thank you for coming in," Lyons said, sitting down alongside Mary Costelloe opposite Tony Fallon.

"We're looking into the sudden death of a Mr Gerald Fortune. I believe he was known to you, is that correct?" Lyons said.

"Fortune the builder. Yeah, you could say that. I did a lot of work for him back in the day, and when the Celtic Tiger stopped roaring he left me high and dry. I lost my business. Had to go to England for a year or two to get back on my feet," Fallon said.

"How much did he leave you short?" Costelloe asked.

"I dunno. Lots. Anyway, that's all over now. I'm working up at the park earning a good wage. I don't want to get back into that game – ever."

"When were you last in touch with Mr Fortune?" Lyons asked.

"God, ages ago. Probably around 2008, or thereabouts. I can't remember."

"But you haven't been in touch recently at all, as in the last month?"

"No, course not. Why do you ask?" Fallon said.

"Where were you on Monday last, Mr Fallon?" Costelloe said.

"I was at work of course."

"And in the evening?" Lyons asked.

"We work late on these summer evenings when it's still light. I didn't finish up till about nine o'clock, and then we went to the pub for a couple of pints before I went home."

"And who were you with in the boozer?" Costelloe said.

"Paddy and Séamus from the job. Look, why are you asking me all this stuff?" Fallon said.

"Tell me, Mr. Fallon, have you ever made any homemade beer, or wine?" Lyons said.

"Jesus! What the hell is going on here? Do I need a solicitor?"

"Just answer the question please, sir," Costelloe said.

"No, I bloody haven't."

"Calm down, Mr. Fallon. You're not in any trouble. We just have to complete our enquiries. Now can you tell me what you did when Mr Fortune left you short of the money he owed you?" Lyons asked.

"I called him. Went round there a few times, but he wouldn't see me. Sent him a few emails. I even got one of your bloody solicitors after him, but all he did was take my money. Useless bugger."

"Is that all? Did you ever threaten Mr Fortune?" Costelloe asked.

"No, of course not. Look, I need to get back to work. Are we done here?" Fallon said.

Lyons opened her folder, and took out a copy of an email that John O'Connor had retrieved from Ger Fortune's archive. She turned the paper around to face Fallon.

"What about this? Looks like a threat to me," she said.

The email didn't make any direct threats against Fortune in terms of bodily harm, but it did contain the rather telling sentence, "You had better not continue to ignore me – I know where you live."

"So?" said Fallon.

"I would consider that a threat if I received it, wouldn't you?" Lyons said.

"No. I was just saying I knew where he lived. It's not a secret. His address is in the phone book," Fallon said.

Lyons said nothing, but her silence spoke volumes as she glared at the man.

"Yes, all right, Mr Fallon. That will be all for now. But we may need to speak to you again, so don't leave town please," Lyons said, taking back the printout of the email and putting it back in the file.

* * *

When Fallon had left, Lyons said to Costelloe, "Mary, can you get back out to Terryland. See if you can find Bolger and get him back here, and talk to the other two blokes that Fallon cited in his statement – check out his alibi."

"Right, boss."

It didn't take Costelloe long to get back out to the forest park, and she was able to drive in and right up to the place where she had collected Fallon earlier. Standing outside, and looking somewhat bewildered, was none other than Inspector James Bolger.

When she got out of the car, Bolger said, "Where the hell did you get to? I've been standing here like a spare for ages. And I didn't find Fallon either."

"It's all sorted. I took him in, and Inspector Lyons has interviewed him. He's on his way back here now, on foot."

"Why the hell didn't you call me to let me know?" Bolger said angrily.

"I tried, but I couldn't. Your phone rang out, and as I had the suspect with me, I thought it best just to bring him in before he took fright and did a runner, sir," Costelloe said.

Bolger searched in his jacket pocket and took out his phone. He shook it a few times before announcing, "Bloody battery is flat. This thing is worse than useless!"

Costelloe tried not to let him see her smiling.

"Well then. We'd better be getting back to Mill Street," Bolger said.

"Not yet, sir. I need to speak to two of Fallon's pals first. They'll be back here in a few minutes for their lunch break," Costelloe said, and she told Bolger about the alibi that Fallon had given.

As Mary Costelloe had predicted, four of the forestry workers came sauntering towards the house a few minutes later.

She identified Paddy and Séamus, and asked about the previous Monday when Fallon had allegedly been drinking with them after a late shift in the park.

"Monday, let's see. I don't think he was with us on Monday, was he, Paddy? No, that's right, he buggered off straight after we'd finished work at six. Said he had something to see to. Didn't see him again till the following morning," Séamus, the self-appointed spokesman for the two men said.

Costelloe made a note in her pocket book before leaving with an even more perplexed James Bolger, and driving back to Mill Street.

Chapter Nineteen

Eamon Flynn called St Begnet's Secondary School from his desk. The phone rang ten times before it was eventually answered.

"Saint Begnet's," a man's voice said rather impatiently.

"Good morning. I wonder if I could speak with Mr Williams if he's available please?"

"Oh, yes, well I'm not sure. I'll have to go and see if I can find him. The school is closed, you know. Who shall I say is calling?" the man said.

"Detective Sergeant Eamon Flynn, thanks."

"Hold on."

Flynn heard the soft thud as the receiver of the telephone was placed on the desk, and he could hear various background noises, and then the distinct sound of a door opening and closing in the distance.

Flynn held on, as directed.

It seemed an age before once again he heard the sound of the door, followed by the sound of the telephone receiver being lifted up again.

"Williams."

"Sorry to trouble you again, but I've been informed that Emma's best friend in school was Amy Cunningham. I'm hoping to speak to Amy a bit later on today, and I was wondering if you would like to come along?" Flynn said.

"Oh yes, well, all right, I suppose. How do you think I can help?"

"Just a friendly face, Mr Williams. I'm sure Amy is not used to dealing with the police, so it may help her to have someone she knows along. Would it be OK if I picked you up in about half an hour?" Flynn said.

"Eh, yes, I suppose so. How long do you think it will take? We're still quite busy here." Williams said.

"Not long. I just want to ask her a few questions, that's all. See you shortly." Flynn hung up rather abruptly as he sensed that the teacher could easily change his mind.

* * *

Amy Cunningham lived with her parents in a much more modest house than the Fortunes. It was a semi-detached one of what James McMahon would have called 'park houses.' The front garden was tidy, but simply laid out, and there was a ten-year-old Volkswagen Golf in the drive which also looked to be in reasonably good condition.

Flynn and Williams got out of Flynn's car, and knocked on the front door, which was a glass panelled affair with the surround painted in a very old-fashioned bottle green. The door was opened by a woman who was probably in her forties, but looked older, with a heavily lined face, and short hair that had once been auburn, but was now yielding to an unflattering grey colour.

Williams greeted the woman as Mrs Cunningham, and introduced Flynn to her.

"Oh, yes, thank you for coming, Mr Williams. Come in, Amy is upstairs, I'll go and get her in a moment. Would you like a cup of tea or coffee gentlemen?"

"No, we're fine, Mrs Cunningham, thanks," Flynn said before Williams had a chance to speak.

Mrs Cunningham showed the two men into the front room of the house, to the left of the hallway. The room was furnished in typical 1980s style, with a patterned floral carpet, and a three-piece suite that had seen better days. The wallpaper was also in a floral pattern, and the well-used fireplace was crafted in local stone with a solid wooden mantelshelf. Despite the rather aged decor, the room was spotlessly clean, and there was a smell of furniture polish in the air.

Mrs Cunningham went upstairs to get her daughter, and a few moments later, Amy came into the room. She had long red hair that was quite unkempt, and a round face dotted with freckles. She was a little on the plump side, but not seriously overweight. Amy was wearing black jeans, with a blue-grey roll neck sweater, and plain slippers. Flynn wondered why teenage girls tended to hang around in twos, where one of them was much prettier than the other. It seemed a common enough phenomenon – he was curious as to exactly what kind of strange symbiosis was at work in these relationships.

Amy said hello to Mr Williams, and Eamon introduced himself, saying how sorry he was for her loss.

"Amy, I'm sorry to bother you, but I was just wondering if Emma ever talked about her father at all?" Flynn asked when they had all sat down.

"Yes, she talked about him all the time – how cool he was, and how generous he always was at birthdays and Christmas, that sort of thing," Amy said.

"Did she ever talk about Mr Fortune's friends, or business acquaintances?"

"No, never."

"Did you ever visit Emma at her home?" Flynn said.

"Yeah, sure. They have a fabulous house. I loved going there. Emma had a cool Bose stereo system. We just have an ancient old system, it's pants," Amy said, rolling her eyes to heaven.

"Did you see Emma's mother at their house?" Flynn said.

"Yes, of course."

"Did you form any opinion of Mrs Fortune?" Flynn asked.

"I'm not sure that's a fair question, Sergeant," Mrs Cunningham said.

"It's OK mum, I don't mind," Amy said, turning to her mother, and then turning back to Flynn. She went on, "she was OK, but I didn't like her that much. She always seemed kinda cold to me. And Emma had some issues with her too. You know Mrs Fortune wasn't her real mother."

"Yes, we know about that. Did you ever see any trouble between Mr and Mrs Fortune – rows or anything, or harsh words?" Flynn said.

"No. I didn't. But he wasn't there much when I was there, like after school and that," Amy said.

"And what about at school," Flynn said, "how did Emma get on with everybody?"

Amy looked down at her shoes, and started to wring her hands together. She had changed her demeanour noticeably in response to Flynn's question.

"Yeah, all fine," she said, and stole a quick, furtive glance at Williams.

Flynn read the signals, and decided not to pursue matters any further with the teacher present.

"Did Emma have a boyfriend, Amy?" Flynn asked.

"No one special. A few of the lads fancied their chances, but she wasn't interested. She said they were all too immature," Amy said.

"I see. And do you have a boyfriend, Amy?"

The girl looked a little nervously at her mother.

"Not really. I've been out with Gavin a few times, but it's not serious."

"OK. Thanks very much Amy, we'll leave it at that for now. You've been very helpful," Flynn said, smiling and getting up. Williams followed his lead, and the two men said their goodbyes and left.

As Flynn drove Williams back to the school, he asked the teacher, "What did you think of that then?"

"She's obviously very distraught. Can't blame her. It's an awful thing to happen."

"Do you think she knows more than she let on?" Flynn said.

"Why do you say that? No, I don't. She's just seventeen for heaven's sake, and her best friend has just died. What did you expect?" Williams said.

"Yeah, you're probably right," Flynn said, but he wasn't convinced.

Chapter Twenty

"Right team," Lyons said as she put her coffee down on the table at the top of the room, "let's hear whatever you've got from today."

Mary Costelloe was first to speak, and this time James Bolger made no attempt to hijack her work.

"We interviewed Fallon and he gave us an alibi for the night before the accident, but it didn't check out, boss. He said he was with his mates in the pub, but they said he took off early," Costelloe said.

"Interesting. I think we'd better get Mr Fallon back in for another little chat, don't you? And this time, let's not be so gentle with him. Make sure you get his fingerprints as well. First thing tomorrow, OK?" Lyons said.

"Yes, boss. No problem," Costelloe said.

"Eamon, did you get to see the Cunningham girl?"

"Yes, I did. There's no doubt she was holding back. She definitely knows something, but I've no idea what. She didn't want to speak up in front of her mother, or Mr Williams for that matter," Flynn said.

"OK. That's a shame, but it could just be some information about weed or something. Emma had some traces in her tox report. We have to be very careful with her, she's underage, and any decent barrister would rip anything we get from her to shreds unless we follow procedure to the letter," Lyons said.

"Eh, boss, she's no longer underage. She was eighteen last week," Fahy said.

"Are you sure, Sally. How do you know?"

"That photograph that the headmaster gave us of the class that Emma and Amy are in. It has all the names and dates of birth on the back. Emma was still seventeen, but Amy turned eighteen last week, so she's technically an adult, and we can question her without an appropriate person present, unless she wants a solicitor," Fahy said.

"I'd still like to go very carefully. If she has something important to tell us we don't want it thrown out on a technicality. Sally, can you see if you can get to talk to her on her own somehow? Offer to take her out for a coffee or something and see what you can get – but by the book, OK?" Lyons said.

"Sure. I'll call her tomorrow morning."

Just then, Sinéad Loughran appeared in the door of the room looking tense.

"Hi, Sinéad, what's up?" Lyons asked, sensing the woman's distress.

"Sorry to interrupt, Inspector, but I thought you should know at once. The plastic tube O'Dwyer took from the Cessna is gone. It was in the evidence room all bagged up and labelled, and it's not there anymore."

"Bloody hell. Has anyone any information on this? Now would be a good time," Lyons said.

The group stirred uneasily in their seats and looked around at each other. After a moment's difficult silence, James Bolger spoke up.

"It's in my car, Inspector," he said.

"And perhaps you could share with us, James, exactly why that is?" Lyons said.

"I was using my initiative, boss. I was going to take it around to the shops in town that sell home brew kits and wine making stuff, and see if anybody recognised it."

"And tell me, James, that you signed it out against your name in the evidence log," Lyons said.

"What log? I didn't know there was one," he said rather sheepishly.

"There is. It's that huge book with the red cover on the shelf by the door with the label 'Evidence Log' stuck on the front of it, and a year's supply of ballpoint pens beside it in the tray."

"Oh, sorry, boss, I didn't know," Bolger said.

A subdued murmur went around the room, but no one laughed out loud.

"Well, perhaps you'd be kind enough to return it as soon as we're finished here," Lyons said.

"Yes, OK. But what about the home brew shops?" Bolger said, not wanting to let go of his idea completely.

"That's not a bad idea. But just go around and get them to give you a list of their regular clients, and see if any names pop up that are involved in this thing. Ask about anyone who bought that type of tubing recently. There's no need to actually take it with you," Lyons said, keen to let her new recruit redeem himself a little in front of the rest of the team.

"And while we're at it, Superintendent Hays had an idea too," Lyons said, looking at Bolger.

"He's curious about what the saboteur did with the proper length of fuel pipe he took from the plane. We've searched all around out at the airport, but there's no sign. And Superintendent Hays suggested we find out from Fergal O'Dwyer what tools you would need to remove the correct fuel line. We know he or she used a screwdriver to tighten the jubilee clips on the plastic pipe, but we didn't find one of those either," Lyons said.

Eamon Flynn spoke up, "That's a good point. And where would the suspect have put the fuel line he removed anyway, if he didn't discard it at the scene?"

"Probably in the boot of his car, if you ask me," Sally Fahy said.

"Agreed," Lyons said, "so we have a good root in the boot of Fallon's car when we bring him in. Now, did we find out about Mrs Fortune's bank accounts?"

"Yes. I had a good go at them earlier. There's nothing strange. A good deal of expenditure in high-end shops, beauty salons, that sort of thing. Then the regular stuff like petrol, parking tags, tolls, but nothing untoward," John O'Connor said.

"Ah, excellent, John. So, can you use your well-honed techy skills to check out where her car was parked on the fateful night? See if we can substantiate her alibi even further, just in case," Lyons said.

"Sure, will do."

"OK. Tasks for tomorrow. James, you can do the rounds of the beer shops and see if that brings up anything? Mary, can you go with Eamon and lift Fallon? Have a good look at his car too while you're at it. Sally, I

137

want you to see if you can get some more from Amy Cunningham. Oh, by the way, John, have you had a peek at Emma Fortune's computer yet?" Lyons asked.

"No, not yet, boss, I haven't had a chance."

"OK. Well, see if you can find time tomorrow. I don't suppose there'll be anything of interest, but you never know. That's it everyone, have a good evening."

As she was packing up her stuff, James Bolger came over to where she was tidying up.

"Can I have a word, boss?" he said.

"Sure, James, what's on your mind?"

"I've been thinking – I don't think I'm really cut out for this job. It's not at all what I expected it to be, and I don't seem to be doing very well at it," he said.

"I see. Well, to be fair, James, you haven't given it much of a chance, have you? It's always a bit rough when you start off – I had a terrible time at first until I got a few collars under my belt. Everyone treated me like the tea girl. You need to give it a proper chance," Lyons said.

"It's not just that. No one respects me. It's like I'm the standing joke around here. I really don't think I can continue."

"Respect, James, has to be earned. Every one of the detectives on my team has had to work hard to prove themselves. Some have made mistakes, and so have I. But after a while it's not the mistakes that are important, it's the triumphs. Those are what people remember. If I were you, I wouldn't hang up your boots just yet. Why not give it another couple of months at least?" she said.

"Well can you at least give me some actual detecting to do then? Going round the shops asking about home brew kits isn't exactly challenging, is it?"

"James, there's something you need to understand about the work that we do. Ninety, no, ninety-five percent of our work is boring hum-drum procedure. Occasionally, the work is punctuated by a few seconds of sheer brilliance that sometimes bears fruit, but mostly it's just dogged persistence that gets us there. It's not like you see on TV, not at all."

Bolger said nothing, but it was clear from his facial expression that he wasn't happy. Lyons sensed his feelings and continued, "Tell you what. Why don't you carry on with this case till we get somewhere with it? That'll make you feel better, and if you're still of the same mind when this is over, I'll have a word with Superintendent Hays and we'll see what can be done?"

"What if we don't solve the case, boss?"

Lyons just looked directly at him, and said nothing.

"Sorry, Inspector. I gather you haven't failed yet. That was thoughtless."

"Go home, James. Do your house calls tomorrow. We'll bring Fallon in and give him a good grilling, and let's see what happens after that. OK?"

"OK, oh, and mum's the word, boss."

"Of course."

Chapter Twenty-one

Lyons nursed her first cup of coffee of the day and busied herself in the office while Mary Costelloe and Eamon Flynn were out collecting Tony Fallon before he could disappear into the undergrowth out at Terryland.

It was 9:40 when the phone on her desk rang.

"Hi. Eamon here, we have him downstairs."

"OK. Great. Have you taken his fingerprints?" Lyons said.

"Mary's doing it now. And you'll love this – we have his car. What a Pandora's box! The boot is jammed with tools of every kind. We've asked Sinéad to come over and deal with it, she knows what she's looking for."

"Nice one. OK. Leave him on his own for about fifteen minutes, then I'll come down. Will you sit in with me?"

"Yes, sure," Flynn said.

"Has he asked for a solicitor?"

"No, no he hasn't."

"But you did caution him?" Lyons said.

"Yes, of course. We did that before we put him in the car in case he said something on the way back we could use. But he stayed shtum."

"OK. See you soon," Lyons said.

* * *

"Look, what's all this about?" Tony Fallon said when Lyons and Flynn entered the room.

"Good morning, Mr Fallon. We'll explain everything in a moment. Have you any idea why you're here?" Lyons said, sitting down opposite the man.

"No, I bloody don't. All I know is you may well have got me fired, so this better be good!"

"Mr Fallon, the last time you were questioned about the untimely death of three people in the plane crash, you told us that on the evening before the accident, you were in the pub with your friends after working late. I have your statement here," Lyons said, opening her folder, and pulling out a copy.

Fallon looked away, but said nothing.

"Would you like to amend that story now?" Lyons said.

Again, Fallon remained quiet, but was clearly becoming uneasy. He was shuffling in his seat, and fidgeting with his hands.

"You see, Mr Fallon, we've checked that out, and it doesn't stack up," Flynn said.

"How do you mean?"

"I think you know very well, Mr Fallon. You weren't in the pub, were you? So that gives us a problem," Lyons said.

Fallon remained silent.

"Just so that you know, while we're sitting here, our forensic team are going over all the tools in your car with a fine-tooth comb. So, is there anything you'd like to tell us at this time?" Lyons said.

Fallon looked straight at Lyons for a few moments, and she held his stare.

"OK, look. You're right, I wasn't in the pub," Fallon said.

"So, where were you and what were you doing?" Flynn asked.

"I was doing a nixer. I'm trying to get back on my feet, so I put down wooden floors for people after hours, but the job can't find out. They expect us to work till sunset in the summer. If they knew I was bunking off, they'd probably fire me," Fallon said.

"And I presume you can give us the name and address of the person you were working for on that occasion?" Flynn said.

"Do I have to? It's all cash in hand work, and I don't want to get anyone into trouble."

"We're not tax collectors, Mr Fallon. We have enough to be doing without all that. But obviously we need to check your story," Lyons said.

Fallon recited the address of a house where he said he was working on the floor on the night in question. Lyons pressed him, and he reluctantly gave up the name and phone number of the householder too.

"Right, Mr Fallon. You need to stay here while we check this out and finish up with your car," Lyons said, tidying up her folder and getting up from the table.

"Can I not go back to work?" Fallon pleaded.

"Mr Fallon, so far, you've lied to the Gardaí and concealed information that could be relevant to our enquiries. So, just sit back and relax, and we'll let you know if you can get back to work, or if we're going to charge you with something," Lyons said, and turned and left the room.

Flynn went off to check Fallon's new alibi with the householder that was having a new floor laid on the cheap, while Lyons caught up with Sinéad Loughran about the car.

"Hi, Sinéad. Anything?"

"Hi Maureen. There're loads of Fallon's prints all over the car, but they don't match the print we got from the lock out at the hangar, or any of the prints on the plane's engine cover. I have two of my folks going through the tools now, but there's no sign of the fuel pipe. Most of this stuff is woodworking kit – chisels, planes, hammer, glue – that sort of thing. Nothing like the tools O'Dwyer described that would be needed to do the job on the plane," Loughran said.

"Shit. OK. Well, keep going. Let me know if you get anything, won't you?" Lyons said.

When she had finished the call, Flynn knocked on Lyons' door.

"Come in, Eamon. What gives?"

"His story checks out. I spoke to a Mrs O'Shea. She confirms Fallon arrived at the house at about six and was there till eleven working on the floor. It's a laminate job, and they're having it fitted throughout the living room, lounge and hall."

"Lovely, I'm sure. Forensics haven't found anything either. Damn! We'll have to let him go. Hang onto him for another hour or so just in case Sinéad comes up with anything, but look after it then, will you?" Lyons said.

"Yes, sure. What now?"

"Let's just hope Inspector Bolger comes back with something."

"Don't hold your breath!" Flynn said, and left the room.

Lyons was stumped. She didn't know which way to turn. They appeared to have virtually no leads now that Fallon was almost certainly going to be cleared of any involvement, and she could feel the pressure mounting for some sort of breakthrough.

In desperation, she called Superintendent Hays.

"Hi, it's me," she said as he answered the phone.

"Hi. How goes it?"

"Shite, to be honest. Are you free for lunch?"

"That bad, eh? Yeah, should be. I have a meeting with Séan Ennis, the guy from Traffic in a few minutes, but that shouldn't take long. I'll stop by and collect you at about half twelve. Does that work for you?"

"Yep! Thanks, Mick."

"No worries, see ya," Hays said.

Chapter Twenty-two

Lyons didn't get to keep her lunch date with her partner. Soon after she had spoken to Superintendent Hays, her phone rang.

"Inspector, it's Sally. I'm out here at the Cunningham's. There's a problem. Amy has disappeared," Fahy said.

"Tell me more," Lyons said.

"I came out to see if I could take Amy out for a coffee or something as you suggested. Her mother said she was still in bed, but she went to get her for me, and found the bed empty. There's no sign of her anywhere. Mrs Cunningham is in bits."

"I bet. Any sign of a note? Has she packed a bag or anything, or can you tell?" Lyons said.

"No note. I don't know if she's taken any clothes or anything, but I'll get her mother to check now."

"OK. Get a recent photo too. I'll put the word out, and then I'll come over. I should be with you in fifteen minutes or so. Hang on in there."

Fahy had managed to get a neighbour to come in to be with Mrs Cunningham, who was, as Fahy had identified earlier, in a bad way. The girl had apparently not packed a bag, nor left any sign of the reason for her sudden departure from the family home.

"When did you see Amy last, Mrs Cunningham?" Lyons asked when she sat down at the kitchen table with Amy's mother, the neighbour, Sally Fahy and the inevitable large pot of tea and cake.

"Last night. She went up to bed after the television news at half past ten, and we assumed she was still there. She sleeps late during the holidays – I rarely see her before noon. But I should have checked on her – it's my fault," Mrs Cunningham said, and her tears began to flow freely again.

The neighbour tried to comfort her friend, with limited success.

Lyons turned to Fahy.

"Has her bed been slept in?"

"She doesn't always make her bed, it seems, so it's hard to tell."

"Hmm, OK. No sign of her phone, I suppose?"

"No. Her mother says she's never without it. I've tried ringing it, but it just goes through to voicemail," Fahy said.

"OK. Well, get the number and phone it through to John O'Connor. See if he can find out where it is now, or when it was last used. And then check with the neighbours – see if they saw anything last night, like a strange car in the road or anything else out of the ordinary," Lyons said.

"Right, boss."

"Mrs Cunningham, did Amy have any other especially close friends, apart from Emma Fortune, I mean?" Lyons asked.

"No. Well, not really. But I've called the only others that she hangs around with, and no one has seen her. God, what are we going to do?"

"To be honest, Mrs Cunningham, we don't usually start a missing person's investigation till someone has gone for at least 24 hours. But I know this is a bit different, given recent events," Lyons said.

"Amy wouldn't just go off like that. That's not her. She's a careful girl. Look, Inspector, you have to find her. Anything could have happened!"

* * *

Hays stopped off at the overflow unit close to Mill Street Garda station to collect Lyons for lunch. When he reached the detective's room, there was hardly anyone there, except for John O'Connor who was working away on a number of computers as usual.

"Hello, John. Is Inspector Lyons here?" Hays said.

"Oh, hello, sir. No, I'm afraid not. She had to dash off a while ago. One of Emma Fortune's friends has gone awol, it seems," the young officer said.

"Oh. Which one?"

"The Cunningham girl, Amy, I think her name is."

"I see. I'll give Maureen a call on her mobile then. Have you made any progress with any of the PCs?" Hays said.

"I'm trying to locate the Cunningham girl's mobile just now, but I managed to get into Emma Fortune's laptop earlier before the sh... sorry, before all this latest fuss started," O'Connor said.

"Anything of interest on it?"

"I'm not sure. I was just getting started on it. It looks like she was fairly active in some sort of chatroom. It's not one that I know much about, but there's a lot of traffic. I'll get a better look at it later if we can find this missing girl."

"Anything I can help with, John?"

"I don't think so, sir. Thanks."

"Right, I'll let you get on then," Hays said, and left the office feeling less connected to real policing than he had in a long time, and he didn't like the feeling – not one little bit.

When Hays had left the office, O'Connor turned his attention in earnest to trying to track Amy Cunningham's phone. He had contacted her airtime supplier, and he was working with them to trace the phone to the nearest transmission mast. The phone had stayed switched on until after 1.30 a.m. and had been pinged at a number of masts leading out of the city. Judging by the rate at which the phone logged on to each successive mast, Amy was being transported by car, and at some considerable speed. The last tower that reported the phone was out west of Moycullen, near Oughterard.

O'Connor left instructions with the phone company to contact him immediately if Amy's phone was turned back on.

Next, he phoned Lyons and relayed the information to her.

* * *

When Lyons got the call from John O'Connor, she went outside the house with Sally Fahy.

"It looks as if Amy has been taken out west. I don't know if she went willingly with someone, or if she's been taken against her will. Get on to Séan Mulholland out in Clifden, and get him to mobilize his resources, and all the other stations in the area. Can you get this photograph of Amy out to him somehow?" Lyons said.

"Yes, I'll take a picture of the photo on my phone and email it to him. I'll get him to set up roadblocks on the N59 and the N341. What are we going to tell the mother?" Fahy said.

"Nothing. Not till we know a bit more."

* * *

Inspector James Bolger arrived back into the Garda station just after lunch. When he found the place virtually deserted, he asked John O'Connor what was going on, and O'Connor brought him up to speed.

"Did you get anything yourself, sir?" O'Connor asked.

"Maybe. I went to all the shops in town that sell home brew stuff, and had a look at their list of regular clients. Amazing. Most of them keep mailing lists so they can send out promo messages when they have a sale on, or something. Only one name came up that we have encountered on this investigation," Bolger said.

"Oh, who's that?"

"Williams, Emma Fortune's form teacher. He's big into wine making it seems and he buys a lot of stuff in McCanns."

"Have you told Inspector Lyons?" O'Connor said.

"Not yet. Do you think I should? I'm sure she's busy enough without me bothering her with trivial details."

"She likes to be kept informed, sir."

"Oh, right. I'll just get a cup of tea, then I'll give her a call."

* * *

Ten minutes later, Bolger called Lyons and told her about what he had found at McCanns.

"It's probably just a coincidence, boss," he said.

"Hmmm. I don't like coincidences, James. Could you give him a call at the school? Just ask him about his wine making hobby. Make up some bullshit to get him talking. Just see how he reacts. And let me know," Lyons said.

Lyons went back inside and explained to Mrs Cunningham that there were now roadblocks arranged in several locations, and all the Gardaí in the area had been alerted to be on the lookout for Amy. She didn't fill the woman in on the information about the last known location of the girl's phone.

Minutes later, James Bolger was back on.

"I called the school, boss. Williams isn't in today. They thought he would be – apparently there are exam papers that need to be corrected this week – but the headmaster explained that once the holidays set in, the teachers mostly come and go as they please, as long as they get the results out on time."

"Ok, well I'd like you to call the school back. Get Williams' address and go round to his house – see if he's at home. If he's there, question him about Amy Cunningham. Everything he knows about her. And keep me posted," Lyons said.

Lyons beckoned Sally Fahy into the lounge out of earshot of Mrs Cunningham and her neighbour.

"I'm going back to the station, Sally, to coordinate things. I'm not sure what's going on, but I have a feeling Amy may be in danger. We need to nip this in the bud before it gets any worse. Will you stay here in case anything breaks, and let me know immediately if it does?"

"Yes. Sure, boss. God, I hope she's OK."

"Me too. See you later," Lyons said, and left.

* * *

On the way back to the station, Lyons tried to figure out what their next move should be. Once again, she was beginning to feel that the situation was slipping away from her. She silently cursed the fact that Hays had been booted upstairs. Then she had an idea.

"Mick, it's me. Sorry about our lunch date, but things took a turn here, and I had to go," she said when she called Hays back at the station.

"Don't mind me – poor starving Superintendent that I am. Anyway, what's happening?"

Lyons explained the latest developments.

"I don't suppose I could drag you away from your precious spreadsheets for a wee while to lend a hand, Superintendent?" she said in a plaintive voice.

"Well, I don't know, Inspector. Security planning for the Taoiseach's visit to the Wild Atlantic Way is pretty important, you know. Yes, of course you can. In fact, I'd be delighted. See you in ten minutes."

When Hays joined her in her office, he asked for a thorough update on the latest developments. As Lyons finished the briefing, her phone rang.

"Inspector, it's James here. I'm out at the school. Williams apparently lives here. He has a small flat upstairs in the main building. It used to be a dormitory once when the school took boarders, but they have converted it, and Williams lives on site." Bolger said.

"Have you been inside the flat yet?"

"Yes, the headmaster opened it up when we couldn't get a reply at the door, just in case he was inside and poorly or something."

"Right. Well, call a uniformed Garda out to stand outside the flat while you come back into town here and get a search warrant. Superintendent Hays can issue it – he's not actively involved on the case yet, but he's here with me. Then get back out there and have a good nosey around. You know what we're looking for – oh, and James, get details of Williams' car and text it to me. I want the reg number, the make, model and colour," Lyons said.

"OK, boss. On my way."

"Do you think Williams is connected to this somehow?" Hays asked.

"It's a bit of a long shot, but definitely a possibility. What do you think?"

"Williams... Williams – what's his first name?" Hays said.

"Let's see. Derek, yes that's it, Derek Williams. Why do you ask?"

"There was a Williams I met in connection with the sailing at the start of the season. I think he said he was a teacher. He bored me to death out at the club one evening with long, uninteresting stories about his own boat. What does this guy look like?" Hays asked.

"He's about 5'9" tall, curly fair hair, cheeky face, average to skinny build."

"Yeah, that sounds about right. Now if only I'd listened a bit harder about his blessed boat. Give me a few minutes and it may come back to me. I'll have to get the search facility on the hard disk in my brain going!"

"Talking of which..." Lyons said.

She called John O'Connor on the internal phone.

"John, could you pop in for a second please?"

Lyons had barely replaced the receiver when John O'Connor appeared in the doorway.

"Hello, Superintendent; Inspector. How can I help?"

"Just wondering if you have got any further with Emma Fortune's PC, John," Lyons said.

"Yes, I have as it happens. She was a big user of this chatroom – BuddySpeak. She talked to some bloke on it nearly every day. Pretty steamy stuff too. But the messages changed in the weeks before the accident. It looks like Emma was changing her mind. She didn't want whatever was going on to continue. I have more work to do to make up a storyboard, and I'm trying to track down his I.P. address at the minute, but he used a proxy server, so it's not straightforward," O'Connor said.

"Any clue as to his identity in any of the messages?" Hays said.

"I'm not sure. There's one message that's signed with several rows of x's and the letter d. It's a capital D. It could be a typo. From the rest of the message, it looks as if the sender might have been a bit drunk, so it's hard to tell."

"Interesting. Another coincidence. That's one too many for me!" Lyons said.

James Bolger was next to appear at her door. Lyons gave Hays a shifty look, and he got the message.

"Just seeing if Inspector Lyons was free for a coffee, James. What can we do for you?" Hays said.

"I'm here to get a warrant to search Derek Williams' rooms out at the school, sir. I believe you can authorize it as long as you're not directly involved with the case," Bolger said.

"Quite correct, Inspector. Give it here, then. I'll sign it."

Bolger handed over the warrant, and Superintendent Hays signed it.

"Now, James, get back out there and see what you can find. Take Mary with you, if you like. This will give you a chance to do some proper detecting," Lyons said.

When he had gone, Hays said, "Proper detecting – what was all that about?"

"He's been giving out that his job is too mundane. I think he thought he was joining CSI or Starsky and Hutch or something when he signed up. He's been talking about leaving – I was supposed to discuss it with you, but I never got the chance," Lyons said.

"It'll keep. Anyway, maybe he'll change his mind with this lot going down," Hays said.

"I hope he doesn't."

Chapter Twenty-three

"Carna, that was it!" Hays said as they sat in the little café across from the station having a coffee. Hays was tucking into a chicken fillet wrap as well, as he had missed his lunch.

"What about Carna?"

"That's where Williams keeps his boat, or at least he did earlier in the summer. Are you thinking what I'm thinking?" Hays said.

"I sure am. Finish your grub and let's go!" Lyons said, draining her coffee cup.

Hays and Lyons collected Eamon Flynn from the station and took a marked squad car from the pool before driving out through the city towards the N59. The city centre was thronged with tourists enjoying the afternoon summer sunshine, and many of them didn't seem to care if they were run over by a speeding Garda car.

Lyons was driving with Hays in the front passenger seat. He was soon on the phone, organising things.

"Pascal, it's Superintendent Hays here. I'm on my way out to you with Inspector Lyons and Sergeant Flynn. I want you to see if you can arrange a boat down at the harbour in Roundstone. We need someone who knows the waters around there well, and a boat that will look fairly inconspicuous – maybe a fishing boat or something. Can you do that?"

"I'll give it a go, Superintendent. How long till you get here?" Brosnan said.

"Probably about forty minutes or so. We'll see you down at the harbour."

"Right. I'd better get busy. See you then."

* * *

Garda Pascal Brosnan ran the small Garda station on the edge of the village of Roundstone single-handedly. He was in his thirties, and although the job could be quite lonely at times, Brosnan got on well with the local community, policing the village with a sensitive but thorough approach. He was familiar with many of the fishermen who eked out a meagre living from their boats and the seas around Bertraghboy Bay.

You wouldn't have known it from the calm summer's day that Brosnan looked out on, but the seas around the village could be vicious, and the boatmen knew, to their cost, just how hard a life fishing in the area could be.

Brosnan made his way down to the first of the two bars opposite the little harbour at Roundstone. Inside, the barman greeted Brosnan warmly.

"Ah, how are ye, Pascal. We don't expect to see you in here at this hour. Are you OK?" the barman said.

"Yes, fine thanks, Shay. Have you seen Paddy Lavelle today?" Brosnan asked.

"I have. Sure, wasn't he here a few minutes ago? That's his pint there on the bar. I think he said he was going across to the shop for a paper. He'll be back in a minute or two. Will you have a drink while you're waiting?" the barman said.

"Ah, no, you're grand. I just want a word with Paddy. I'll stroll across and catch him outside," Brosnan said.

Paddy was walking back across the road reading the front page of the paper when Brosnan approached.

"Hello there, Paddy. Listen, I have three colleagues on their way out from the city. They were wondering if you'd take them out in your boat. They want to go across Carna way," Brosnan asked.

"I suppose I could, all right. Would this be official Garda business now?" the old timer said.

"I imagine it is. Oh, I see what you're getting at. I'm sure we can get you a tankful of diesel at least out of it. But let's see how we get on. I'll see you down there in a few minutes, good man, Paddy."

* * *

James Bolger returned to the school armed with his search warrant and showed it to Donal O'Connell, the headmaster.

"Is this all really necessary, Inspector? I have no objection to you having a look around Mr Williams' rooms. There's no need for that."

"We have to do everything by the book, headmaster. Now, excuse me, I must get on."

Bolger and Costelloe donned blue vinyl gloves, and started searching Derek Williams' rooms. Bolger found a laptop computer on a coffee table in the living room and placed it in a large evidence sack, labelling it in black felt pen. Mary Costelloe searched the bedroom, and found little of interest. Then she opened a door to the left of the hall that gave into a small, dark room that looked as if it might have been a pantry at some stage. She switched on the light, and found one of the shelves packed with home wine making equipment. There was a demi-john filled with a deep ruby-coloured liquid on the largest shelf, with a plastic air lock stuck in the top of it, and beside it, Mary spotted a coil of clear plastic tubing.

Costelloe called Bolger to share her discovery with him.

"Take this back in an evidence bag to Sinéad Loughran in town, and get her to see if there is a match to the tubing recovered from the aeroplane. Don't handle it more than you have to. Off you go now," he said rather condescendingly.

Bolger called Lyons on her mobile, and she answered using the Bluetooth hands-free in the squad car.

Bolger updated Lyons with the latest developments.

"Thanks, James. Get the PC back to John O'Connor and get him to prioritize it. See if he can match it to Emma's computer. I don't understand all that mumbo-jumbo, but he'll know what to do," Lyons said.

"Right, boss. What are you up to?"

"Oh, we're just going to do a spot of fishing out near Roundstone, see you later." She hung up before Bolger had a chance to ask anything more.

* * *

Lyons drove the squad car up to the car park opposite the Roundstone House Hotel. She didn't want to draw attention to the fact that they were intending to set to sea, although in fairness, she guessed that it would be all around the town by evening.

Down at the harbour, Paddy Lavelle had the engine on his fishing boat going, and pale blue diesel smoke was rising up out of the rusty pipe that ran up the side of the wheelhouse into the clear air above.

The boat was an old wooden boat, but Paddy maintained it in reasonable condition, and it had a fairly fresh coat of navy-blue paint on the hull, finished in white along the gunwales. Forward of the wheelhouse there was a chain locker set into the deck, where the anchor chain was stored, and there was another hatch that opened into a large storage area below decks that could be used to store freshly caught mackerel.

Behind the wheelhouse, on the main deck of the boat, the rusty paraphernalia of sea fishing was stacked: a tangle of wire, netting and large iron pieces, each with its own special purpose. A few dirty fish boxes were piled on top of each other in the corner at the stern, smelling rather ripe. The boat rose and fell gently on the waves, its rubber fenders squeaking against the harbour wall from time to time.

"Well done, Pascal, this is just the ticket," said Hays, patting the younger Garda on the upper arm.

It was decided that Pascal, the only uniformed officer amongst them, should remain on dry land and co-ordinate efforts via the radio. He had a small but powerful hand-held set, and Paddy assured them that the boat's radio was in good working order.

"We'll use channel 44, Paddy, unless an emergency develops," Brosnan said to the boatman.

"Right so, where are we off to?" Lavelle asked.

"We want to head out towards Carna, Paddy. How long will it take us to get to Carna Bay?"

"The tide will be with us on the way over, so not more than an hour at most, I'd say."

"When we get close in, is there somewhere the two of us can hide on board, Paddy?" Lyons asked.

"There is. There's a galley below. It's small, but two can fit in there handy enough, and you'll be right out of sight," Lavelle said.

"Grand, thanks, Paddy. Let's get going," Hays said.

They untied the boat, and Paddy manoeuvred it deftly out of the tiny harbour as he had done thousands of times before. There was a gentle swell on the sea as they crossed Bertraghboy Bay, and occasionally a wisp of spray was thrown up over the bow of the little boat and splashed on the windows of the wheelhouse.

When they reached the more open sea out of the lea of the land, the swell increased a bit, and Eamon Flynn began to feel decidedly queasy. It wasn't long before he was leaning out over the side of the boat retching up his lunch, much to the amusement of the skipper who had the good sense to say nothing.

The little vessel ploughed on, and after three quarters of an hour, they rounded the headland guarding the entrance to Carna Bay. Lyons used the boat's radio to check in with Brosnan.

She rotated the knob on the front of the radio till the number 44 was illuminated in green figures on the display. She pressed the button on the side of the microphone and said, "Lyons to Brosnan. How do you read, over?"

"Brosnan to Lyons. I read you well, boss. Over."

"Standby on this channel, Pascal. We're just entering Carna Bay now, over."

"Any sign of the target? Over," Brosnan asked.

"Negative. Not yet anyway. I'll let you know, over."

When Paddy Lavelle's boat got into the shelter of the land, the sea became quite calm, and he brought back the throttles, so that the vessel moved more slowly in towards Carna. A sailing boat, anchored well off the coast, came into view. It was a single-masted yacht with the mainsail stowed along the boom, and the foresail furled around the forestay, with the sheets leading back to the cockpit.

"It looks as if he has it set up for single-handed sailing," Hays said.

"Can you get between him and the shore, and approach him from the leeward side?" Hays asked.

"I surely can. Are you planning on boarding her?"

"Yes, I am."

"Better put out the fenders, then. I wouldn't want to scratch her paintwork now, would I?" Paddy said.

Lyons took the hint, and went out on deck to push the large plastic fenders over the side of the boat on the starboard side.

When she was back in the cramped wheelhouse, Hays said, "Can you go below with Eamon in case Williams is keeping a lookout."

"Hmm, OK, but if he pukes all over me, you'll be doing the laundry," Lyons said.

As she turned to leave the wheelhouse, Hays gave her a friendly pat on the rear. She smiled to herself as she struggled to lower herself backwards down the steep metal ladder into the bowels of the boat. Once they were actually down there, it was roomier than they had been led to believe, and was surprisingly tidy and neat. There was a two-ring gas stove, gimballed, so it could be used as the boat rocked about at sea; a small gas-powered fridge, like the ones you see in caravans, and a tiny circular sink. A hinged table could be lifted out and secured against the floor that allowed two people to sit and eat. A round opaque glass light fitting was mounted in the ceiling that shed sufficient brightness into the room to allow for the preparation of simple food in the galley.

As Lavelle skilfully brought the fishing boat alongside the sloop, Hays stood up on the gunwale and reached out to grab the shroud of the sailing boat. He transferred his weight to the gunwale of the yacht, and swung his legs over the handrails one at a time, to land on the deck forward of the cockpit.

Boarding the sailing boat in this way had caused it to heel over considerably, and as Hays went aft towards the hatch, it opened and the top half of Derek Williams appeared in the companionway.

"What the fuck's going on, and who the hell are you?" Williams said.

Hays produced his warrant card, and introduced himself.

"You've no right to board my boat. Get off, before I throw you off. I know my rights," Williams blustered.

"I don't think so, Mr Williams," Hays said, gesturing towards the fishing boat alongside, where Lyons and Flynn had emerged on the deck.

"Now, I want you to let me pass, Mr Williams. I need to see inside your yacht," Hays said.

"No chance. This is private property, now piss off and leave me alone."

Hays put his hand behind his back, and waved slightly at the two detectives on the other boat. Lyons read the signal, and turned away, taking Flynn by the arm, and turning him away too. Then Hays lifted his foot, and gave Williams a firm push in the chest. The man fell backwards with a yelp and slid along the floor. Before he could get up, Hays jumped down into the cabin and brought his foot to rest just below Williams' neck.

"Thank you for inviting me on board, sir," Hays said, looking around, examining the inside of the spacious craft.

"What's through that door, Williams?" Hays asked, nodding towards a closed wooden door in the forward end of the yacht.

"Nothing, just an empty cabin."

Hays, still keeping his foot on the prone form of the teacher on the floor, turned and shouted out through the open hatch, "Come aboard, Inspector; Sergeant."

He felt the boat sway under his feet as the two Gardaí boarded the boat following Hays' example. Hays reached out to a shelf that ran along the length of the cabin to steady himself.

"Look, can I get up now please?" Williams asked.

"No, not yet. In a minute."

As the two other detectives came down the steps, Hays said to Flynn who was in front, "Sergeant, look after Mr Williams for me."

Williams scrambled up and sat on the bench seat at the side of the cabin. Hays went forward and tried to open the end door, but it was locked.

"I need this open, Mr Williams," Hays said.

"I told you, there's nothing in there, it's empty," Williams protested.

"I've had enough of this," Hays said losing patience. He took a step forwards, raised his foot to knee height, and kicked the door hard. The wood splintered at the lock, and the door flew back on its hinges.

"Christ," exclaimed Williams.

As the door flew open, the girl that was lying on the bed, gagged with gaffer tape, with her hands tied behind her back, looked at Hays with pure terror in her eyes.

"It's OK, love, I'm with the police. You're safe now. It's over. Maureen, in here," he said loudly, turning towards the broken door. Lyons came in to attend to the girl.

Hays turned back to the cabin where Williams was sitting on the settee with his hand in his head.

"Eamon, arrest him on suspicion of abduction, kidnap, assault, being a prick – anything else you can think of. Cuff him, and get him on board the fishing boat. Try not to drop him in the sea, but not too hard. I've a good mind to put him in the fish hold," Hays said.

Lyons had untied Amy Cunningham's wrists, and carefully removed the gaffer tape from her mouth. She was holding the girl around the shoulders, and Amy was sobbing uncontrollably as she buried her head in Lyons' shoulder.

When Flynn had manhandled Williams onto the other vessel, without dropping him in the sea, Hays said to Lyons, "We'll take this boat back into Roundstone. We can follow Paddy. Can you get on the radio? Ask Pascal to get Sinéad out. We'll need her to take fingerprints, and whatever samples she can get off the sheets on that bed. And tell him to lock Williams up in a cell till we get back."

"OK. I'm on it," Lyons said.

Chapter Twenty-four

Hays made his way to the front of the yacht and used the windlass on the foredeck to bring up the anchor, stowing the long chain in the locker provided. Williams had left the key in the ignition switch, and Hays started the engine on the first turn of the starter. He engaged forward on the gear selector, and advanced the throttle. The yacht came around under his direction, and fell in behind the wash from Paddy's fishing boat, heading for Roundstone.

Amy Cunningham was feeling a bit better once the yacht was underway. Maureen Lyons fetched her a drink of water, and the girl had stopped crying. Lyons used her radio to call Pascal Brosnan, and asked him to contact the Cunninghams and tell them that Amy had been found safe and sound. Lyons wasn't quite sure about the last bit, but it would do for now in any case.

When they reached Roundstone, the weather was noticeably cooler as evening set in. Hays brought the yacht alongside a blank spot against the harbour wall and tied it off forward and aft, leaving enough rope to ensure that the boat wouldn't hang itself when the tide went out.

Lyons helped Amy up the slippery metal ladder built into the side wall of the harbour.

In the time it had taken them to motor back to Roundstone, Sinéad Loughran had arrived out with another forensic officer to examine Williams' boat. As soon as Lyons, Hays and Amy had disembarked, Loughran took over the boat. She wrapped it in blue and white Scene of Crime tape, and went on board with the second forensic investigator.

Brosnan had taken Williams away to lock him up in the local Garda station, leaving Flynn standing on the dock. Hays asked Flynn if he had found out where Williams had left his car.

"I asked him all right. You'll never guess what he said," Flynn said.

"Go on," Hays said.

"'You're the fucking detective – you find it!'"

"Charming! Right," Hays said, "let's get you back home, Amy, Inspector Lyons will go with you. We'll need to talk to you tomorrow about all of this, but we'll leave it for tonight, let you get over your ordeal."

* * *

It was nearly nine o'clock by the time Lyons arrived home to the house she shared in Salthill with Mick Hays. Hays had taken a tray meal for two out of the freezer, and when Lyons came in, he put it in the oven to cook.

"How long will that take?" she asked, giving him a kiss on the cheek as she took off her coat.

"Half an hour or so," Hays said.

"Great, I'm going to have a quick shower – I stink of dead fish! Have we a nice bottle of red?"

"Yep, I'll dig something out."

Half an hour later they sat and ate the meal, washed down with a bottle of Montepulciano D'Abruzzo that Hays had found in the sideboard.

"Mmm, that's a lovely wine," Lyon said.

"I must try and get some more of it. It wasn't even that dear – about twelve euro if I remember rightly."

"Thanks for your help today, by the way. I was beginning to feel a bit out of my depth," Lyons said.

"No trouble. But in fairness, you had it more or less under control all along. I didn't do much," Hays said.

"I'm not much good at breaking down doors, Mick. And I loved the way you kicked Williams in the boat. Very macho!"

"Oh, you'd have got him just the same. Remember Lorcan McFadden? Not to mention the bank robber on Eyre Square. You haven't let one slip through your fingers yet, kiddo."

"Still, it was good to have you along. I dunno – I just feel so much more confident when we're working together. Oh, and by the way, what are we going to do about Bolger?" Lyons said.

"I'll talk to him over the next few days. Do you want him on the team?"

"Not really. Is that terrible? We'd better be careful not to upset Plunkett though."

"Don't worry about that. I'll convince Finbarr that the force would be much better served if we were exploiting Mr Bolger's cerebral talents. We'll get him a nice desk job doing research or something," Hays said.

"Do you think that will fly, Mick?"

"I'll make it fly if that's what you want."

"It might be best. He doesn't fit in, and some of the team think he's just a joke. I don't think he's happy either. Probably the right thing to do if you could move him on."

* * *

Williams was brought into the city early the following morning. The detectives were conscious that they only had a limited time to question him, and from experience, they knew that it could fly by amazingly quickly.

It had been decided that Hays and Flynn would interview Derek Williams, and that Lyons and Fahy would deal with Amy Cunningham. Lyons asked James Bolger to assist John O'Connor with the computer stuff, to see if real evidence of a connection between Emma Fortune and her form teacher could be established.

While the two female detectives went out to the Cunningham's house to bring Amy into the station, Hays and Flynn got busy with the teacher.

Amy Cunningham was up and dressed and having breakfast with her mother in the kitchen when Lyons and Fahy arrived. Mrs Cunningham invited them in, and offered them tea and toast, which they gratefully accepted.

"We'd like to thank you so much for getting Amy back safely, Inspector. What's going to happen to that terrible man?" Mrs Cunningham said.

"We have him in custody for now, Mrs Cunningham. My colleagues are interviewing him as we speak," Lyons said.

"Amy, we'd like you to come with us to Mill Street, if you wouldn't mind. We need to get a statement from you about the events of the last couple of days, if that's all right?" Fahy said.

"Do I have to come in today?" Amy said rather shakily, looking to her mother.

"That would be best, Amy. You see, we need your statement to charge Mr Williams – otherwise we'll just have to let him go this evening, and we'd rather that didn't happen," Fahy said.

"Oh, I see. Well, can my mum come with me?" the girl said.

"I don't see why not. Why don't you get ready, and we can go in our car?" Lyons said.

They cleared the breakfast things into the kitchen sink, and Mrs Cunningham disappeared for a few minutes, reappearing with her make up done and her hair neatly brushed.

When they got to the station, the two detectives took Amy into the nicer of the interview rooms and arranged a soft drink for her, and coffees for themselves.

"Now, Amy, thanks for coming in. I just want to say you're not in any trouble here. We just need to get to the bottom of things, so if some of the questions we ask seem a bit strange, please bear with us. Is that OK?" Lyons said.

"Yes, I suppose so," Amy said.

"Right then. Let's start with how you ended up on the boat. Tell us what happened," Lyons said.

"Well, the other night, I had gone up to bed at about ten, I think, when I got a text message on my phone. It was Mr Williams. He said he needed to see me, and that it was important. I replied saying I would contact him the next day, but he came back and said, no, he needed to see me that evening, and told me not to say anything to anyone. He said it was something to do with Emma."

"Do you still have that string of messages on your phone, Amy?" Fahy asked.

"I don't know, I think so. My phone is in my coat outside. Do you want me to go and get it?"

"Not just now, we can get it later. So, what happened then?"

"I got dressed and sneaked out of the house without Mum and Dad hearing me, and I went to meet Mr Williams at the entrance to the lane that runs behind our houses. That's where he asked me to be."

"And when you got there?" Lyons said.

"He asked me to get into his car, so I did. We drove out a bit into the country. He wasn't saying anything, so I asked him what it was all about, but he wouldn't say. Then he stopped the car in an entrance to a field, and reached over and put that tape on my mouth. I tried to get out of the car, but he was too strong, and he had these plastic things that he put around my wrists. He told me to stop struggling or he'd have to hurt me. It was awful." Amy started to cry as she recounted what had happened to her.

Lyons gave her a few moments to compose herself and handed her some tissues from a box that was on the table.

"I know this is difficult, but can you tell us what happened next?" she asked.

"We drove off again. He was driving very fast, and eventually we came to this little place down by the sea. He had his boat there, and he got me out of the car and pushed me on board. He locked me in the bedroom, and then he started up the boat and set off out to sea," Amy said.

"Why do you think he did this, Amy?" Fahy asked.

Amy looked down at the floor, and said nothing for a minute or two, but then lifted her eyes and said, "I know things about him and Emma."

"What sort of things?" Lyons asked.

"You know. Bad things. But I don't want to say. It was a secret we shared."

"Amy, you can't do anything to hurt Emma now. She was your best friend. Don't you think she deserves your honesty at this stage if it will help bring the killer to justice?" Lyons said.

"Yes, but Mr Williams didn't kill her – he couldn't have. He was in love with Emma. They were having an affair!" the girl said.

"I see. And how long had this been going on, Amy?"

"About two years. It started when we were on a hockey trip to Derry. That was the first time. She was so excited," Amy said.

"So, you're saying that this so-called affair started when Emma was just fifteen?"

"Well, yes, but it wasn't like that. She was really in love with him, till… till…"

"Till what, Amy?" Lyons said.

"Emma found out he was sleeping with one of the other girls. She was devastated. Of course, she broke it off with him at once. Told him where to go. And she said she was going to tell her parents. That would have put the cat among the pigeons, wouldn't it?"

"Yes, I should imagine it would. Had she actually told them yet?" Fahy said.

"No, I don't think so. No, she mustn't have. I would have heard about it. But she was going to. She said so. Don't you believe me?" Amy asked, getting a little agitated.

"Yes, of course. We just need to get as much detail as we can, Amy. You're doing really well," Lyons said.

Chapter Twenty-five

Williams had asked for a solicitor, which delayed the start of the interview that Hays and Flynn wanted to get started on. But it wasn't all bad, as the extra time gave John O'Connor longer to try to establish a link between Williams' and Emma Fortune's computer, and Sinéad Loughran longer to work on the forensic evidence from the boat and from the material collected from Williams' rooms at the school.

At half past ten, a Mr Ernest Joyce, Williams' solicitor, presented at the station and asked to see his client. Hays had encountered Joyce previously, and deemed him to be a reasonable sort, given his chosen profession, although he was inclined to be a bit too thorough for Hays' liking. Such thoroughness rarely favoured the Gardaí when they were trying to get a confession.

By eleven o'clock, Hays was getting impatient, and decided to get things moving. He collected Flynn from the open-plan, and they went together to the shabbier of the two interview rooms where Williams had been brought.

"Good morning, Mr Williams, I trust you spent a comfortable night?" Hays said, sitting down opposite the man who looked anything but comfortable.

"I want to make a formal complaint. You assaulted me yesterday after you came aboard my boat without permission. That's piracy you know?" Williams said.

"Eamon, you were there, did you see me assault the suspect?" Hays said.

"No, sir, I didn't. All I saw was Mr Williams on the floor of the cabin. He must have lost his footing when the boat hit a wave," Flynn said.

"And as for piracy, Mr Williams, you need to study your marine law a bit more. Now, can we stop this nonsense and get on," Hays said.

"What exactly are you intending to charge my client with, Superintendent?" Joyce said.

"For the moment, abduction. But further charges may follow as we continue with our investigations."

"And I presume you have evidence of this alleged abduction," Joyce said.

"We have a statement from the girl who was abducted telling how your client put gaffer tape across her mouth, bound her wrists with plastic tie-wraps, and forced her onto his yacht where we both found her in a locked cabin yesterday. Will that do?" Hays said.

"Come now, Superintendent. That all sounds like the imaginative fantasy of an impressionable schoolgirl to me."

"Mr Williams, do you deny asking Amy Cunningham to meet you two nights ago late into the evening when she was at home getting ready for bed?" Hays said.

"Yes, of course I do. That's nonsense. It was she who demanded that I call round to see her. The girl obviously has a crush on me," Williams said.

Hays said nothing, but he opened the folder he had brought with him into the room, removed the transcript of the text message that Williams had sent Amy and turned it around to show Williams.

"We have Amy's phone, Mr Williams, and we'll be able to get your text messages off it easily enough later this morning, so it would be better if you told the truth," Hays said.

Williams looked at Joyce who shook his head imperceptibly, and neither of them spoke.

"So, can you tell us, Mr Williams, why you abducted Amy Cunningham?" Hays asked.

"No comment," came the reply.

Hays stared at the man for a moment, and then tapped Flynn under the table.

"Mr Williams, how well did you know Emma Fortune?" Flynn asked.

"I knew her. She was in my form class, and she was on a couple of the sports teams that I help out with at the school."

"Did you like Emma?" Flynn said.

"Yes, I suppose so. Not any more than any of the other pupils. But she was nice enough," Williams said.

"Mr Williams, isn't it true that you had a relationship with Emma Fortune – a sexual relationship, and that this had been going on since she was fifteen?" Flynn said.

"What? That's nonsense. You can't go around accusing people of things like that – it's preposterous!" Williams shouted, looking plaintively at his lawyer.

Joyce remained cool.

"I presume, Sergeant, you have some evidence to back up this nonsensical fairy tale?"

"Are you denying it then, Mr Williams?" Flynn said.

"Of course I'm bloody denying it. It's ridiculous. What sort of man do you think I am?"

"I need a comfort break, and I suggest Mr Joyce that you talk to your client and advise him to start cooperating with us, for his own good. Shall we say half an hour?" Hays said, getting up and signalling to Flynn to leave with him.

The two detectives returned to the open-plan office where Lyons was chatting to Fahy over a cup of tea.

"How did it go with the girl?" Hays asked.

"Oh, fine. She gave us a statement that should wrap up the abduction charge anyway. We sent her home, she's pretty shook up still. Oh, and she told us that Williams was having sex with Emma too, but that Emma had dumped him recently and was threatening to tell tales. Apparently, it started when she was just fifteen," Lyons said.

"Charming. Still, that's only hearsay until we get some evidence. If we can't link Williams to the plane crash, and so far, we haven't any hard evidence to lay before him, we'll have to charge him with the abduction, and get him in front of a judge," Hays said.

"Christ, are you serious, sir? Surely we have enough to hold him a bit longer. Sinéad is working flat out to try and link all the evidence up," Fahy said.

"We have to be careful. Joyce has already said he's not happy about the warrant for the search on Williams' place. He's going to try and make the case that I was involved when I issued the warrant. If he succeeds with that, then anything we found out there would be inadmissible. I think our best bet is to charge him with the abduction, then get him before the court and make sure he is remanded. That way we'll have a lot more time to get our ducks in a row and bring further charges as appropriate," Hays said.

"Do you think he did it?" Fahy asked.

"Well, there's a pretty strong motive there if what Amy said is true. Opportunity too, and maybe even the means. That reminds me, has anyone told the headmaster about Williams yet?" Hays said.

"No, I don't think so," Lyons said, looking around to see if the others could confirm.

"OK. Sally, can you chase up John and Sinéad. Eamon, I'd like you to go back in for round two with Williams in half an hour or so. See if you can shake anything more out of him. Then, if there's nothing new, just charge him with the abduction. Maureen, you and I are going back to school!"

* * *

"Hi John," Sally Fahy said, "how's it going?"

"Slowly, Sarge. I'm making headway, but it's slow work. I have Emma's side of things pretty well broken down now, but Williams' PC is much harder. I'm sure there's plenty of traffic between them in there, I just need a few more hours to prove it," O'Connor said.

"OK. Well if you get anything, let us know at once. We can't hold him much longer and he's got Ernest Joyce acting for him."

"Right, I'll let you know if I get anything."

Next, Fahy rang through to Sinéad Loughran.

"Hi Sinéad, it's Sally. The boss wants to know if you've got any evidence that could tie Williams to Emma Fortune?"

"We're not sure yet, Sally. We recovered some hair from the bed out on the boat that isn't Amy's. I'm having it checked at the moment against Emma's. The first examination will be just under a microscope. But to get anything that would stand up in court, we'll need a DNA match. That will take a few days. That's about it, I'm afraid," Loughran said.

"Did you get anywhere with the fuel pipe and the wine making kit?" Fahy said.

"I haven't got round to that stuff yet. But I'll get to it this afternoon and let you know if I find anything. Now I must get on."

"Yes, sorry, of course. Talk later, bye."

* * *

Hays and Lyons found the headmaster in his study at the school. The place had a more deserted feel to it now, as many of the staff had left for their holidays, but Donal O'Connell appeared to be well occupied with paperwork of various kinds.

"May we come in, Mr O'Connell," Lyons said, knocking on the headmaster's door.

Hays introduced himself and Lyons to the man, presenting his business card and shaking hands.

"My, my, a Superintendent, no less. This must be important," O'Connell said. "Come in, sit down. Sorry I can't offer you a cup tea or coffee – catering's finished for the summer I'm afraid. Now how can I help you?"

Hays explained that they had Mr Derek Williams in custody, and that he was going to be charged with the abduction of one of the school's pupils, explaining that Williams had essentially kidnapped young Amy Cunningham.

"Oh, but that's terrible. Are you certain that he is involved?"

"Yes, we are, Mr O'Connell, and I'm sorry to say there may be further charges to follow," Lyons said.

"Really. What sort of charges?"

"We're not in a position to say at the moment, but it's quite serious."

"Heavens, I had no idea that anything like this was going on. Are there any other pupils involved?"

"Perhaps. As I say, we're not in a position to reveal any more information at this time," Lyons said.

"Gracious, I suppose I should contact Mr and Mrs Cunningham, although what on earth I'm going to say to them, I don't know. Is Amy all right?"

"She's a bit shook up, but she wasn't harmed, if that's what you mean," Hays said.

"Well, yes, that's something I suppose," O'Connell said.

"Mr O'Connell, I'm sorry to have to ask you this, but were there any signs at all that Mr Williams might be getting, shall we say, over familiar with any of the girls?"

"No, not that I am aware of, in any case. You have to understand that as headmaster, I'm not always privy to all the gossip in the staffroom. The other staff tend to keep their distance somewhat," O'Connell said, but he was avoiding eye contact as he said it, so Lyons pressed on.

"Did Mr Williams ever take any of the pupils on school outings – you know like sporting fixtures and the like?" she said.

"Yes, well, from time to time, he did. He is very supportive of the girls' hockey team. He spends a lot of his free time coaching them and arranging games. To be honest, we'd be lost without him."

"And can you remember if Mr Williams ever went with the team to Derry?" Lyons said.

"I don't recall specifically, but I imagine he would have done. That's an annual event we have with a Protestant school there – a sort of 'hands across the border' sort of thing. Unfortunately, they usually beat us," the headmaster said, smiling.

"I wonder if you could check that for us please, Mr O'Connell, it's quite important."

O'Connell was looking more uneasy as the conversation went on, but he turned around to face the row of old green filing cabinets behind him, and opened a drawer low down in the third one from the left. He withdrew a well-worn folder and brought it to the desk.

Hays and Lyons remained silent as O'Connell thumbed through the many sheets of paper in the file, till at last he pulled out two yellow printed pages, and placed them on top of the rest.

"Yes, here we are. Mr Williams' expense claims for the hockey team's trip to Derry. It seems he conducted the outing for the past two years."

"And may we have a list of the pupils that went on those journeys please, Mr O'Connell?" Lyons asked.

The man went back into the file and rummaged some more, before retrieving a few dog-eared sheets of white paper. Lyons could read the words upside-down in large letters at the top of the uppermost sheet, 'Girls' Under 18 Hockey Team – Eglington School, Derry', with several names listed beneath, and details of the timings for the departure and return journey. The pages had pin holes in each corner, presumably where they had been displayed on some notice board or other around the school.

"I can give you a copy of these, if that would help. Is there anyone in particular you are interested in?"

Lyons looked at Hays who gave a tiny nod.

"Yes, there is, sir. Can you tell me if Emma Fortune was on those teams?" Lyons said.

O'Connell scanned both pages again.

"Yes, she was on the team on both occasions. Here, look," he said, turning the paper around and pointing with his pen to the name.

"May I ask what the significance of your enquiry is?" O'Connell said.

Hays thought for a moment, and then decided that as they had Amy Cunningham's statement now, he could give the headmaster a clue as to the direction their enquiries were going.

"There has been a suggestion that there may have been some impropriety involving Mr Williams and Emma Fortune during one or perhaps both of those excursions, Mr O'Connell," Hays said.

O'Connell sighed, looking down at his desk. After a moment of silence, he spoke again.

"Look, I'm afraid I haven't been totally honest with you. There was an incident that might support what you are suggesting. I was called to the classroom of our Mrs Wallace – she's the senior English teacher – during winter term last year. Someone had put some graffiti on her blackboard during the break. It had Derek and Emma chalked up in big letters with a heart in between their names, and unfortunately a rather crude drawing of some male private parts beneath. Mrs Wallace was very upset," O'Connell said, shuddering slightly at the recollection.

"I see. And what action did the school take?" Lyons asked.

"We asked Mr Williams about it, but of course he denied everything, so we put it down to schoolgirl high jinks and left it at that. There were rumblings in the staffroom for a while afterwards, but it eventually died down."

The headmaster rubbed his face with both hands, and sat back in his chair.

"I suppose I'd better get the school's solicitor on stand-by," O'Connell said in an exasperated fashion. Clearly, he wasn't used to having to deal with such matters.

Chapter Twenty-six

Back at the station, Flynn had had another go at Williams, but made no further progress. Ernest Joyce, the solicitor, was emboldened following the departure of Superintendent Hays, and insisted that his client be either charged or released. Flynn obliged by charging Williams with abduction, and as luck would have it managed to get the man before Judge Meehan just as he was finishing up for the day.

In the courtroom, before Judge Meehan, Joyce made a big fuss about his client's innocence, the fact that he was a school teacher, and hence an upstanding member of the community and, of course, had a blemish-free record to date. Flynn responded with an account of the abduction of Amy Cunningham, and the judge was persuaded that there was enough to bring charges against the man, but Flynn could see that the judge was uncomfortable. At the end of the hearing, Joyce broached the subject of bail.

Flynn applied for a remand on the basis that he believed Williams to be a flight risk, but Meehan would have none of it. He rattled on about a man of good character being innocent until proven guilty, and that depriving a man of his liberty was a serious matter. He did however impose conditions on the accused, telling him that he must surrender his passport, report to the Gardaí twice weekly, and under no circumstances was he to make any contact by any means with any of the witnesses in the case – specifically, Amy Cunningham. The judge made it quite clear that in the event of any breach of these conditions, he would be re-arrested and held on remand until his trial.

Williams was sullen in the court room, but brightened up quickly on hearing that he was to be released, and thanked Joyce profusely on the steps of the court before disappearing into the city.

* * *

On the way back from the school in the car, Lyons asked Hays what he thought of the headmaster's performance.

"Well, he was clearly aware of Williams' tendencies, even if he didn't know any of the details. But I suppose when you have someone who appears dedicated to their work, and goes the extra mile, you're inclined to overlook some aspects of their less professional behaviour. A bit like me with you," Hays said.

"Cheeky bugger," she said, giving him a hard slap on his thigh.

"But in my experience, schools are a hotbed of rumour, gossip and intrigue of all sorts. They can be quite detached from reality, and all caught up in their own little world. I'm sure lots and lots goes on that we never hear about," Hays said.

* * *

Back at the station, they brought everyone together to see what developments had happened while they were out at the school.

There was little to be reported. The team were quite despondent that they had had to let Williams go, and that the judge had seen fit to release the school teacher on bail, but there was nothing that they could have done about it. They simply didn't have enough to charge him with anything further, and while Eamon Flynn had done his best with Judge Meehan, saying that there would likely be further charges to be brought in due course, the law was the law, and the man had to be released.

"I have a feeling Meehan may know the accused. They might even know each other socially to some extent. Galway is a small town, don't forget," Flynn said.

"Has anyone been in touch with Sinéad?" Lyons asked, taking charge of the meeting.

"Yes, boss," Sally Fahy said, "but she says we have to be patient. She's getting the hair samples from the boat analysed, as well as the sheets – she says there are signs of a lot of bodily fluids on them – and they are bringing in an expert to look at the two samples of plastic tubing too. But it will be tomorrow at least before she has anything useful to tell us."

"Thanks, Sally. Anybody else got anything?" Lyons said.

An uneasy silence pervaded the room.

"Right, well then, if there's nothing else, you can all get back to work. I presume we're keeping an eye on Williams?"

"I've advised Amy Armstrong – or should I say her mother – that Williams has been released on bail, and if she sees him, or if he attempts to make contact, she should call us at once," Eamon Flynn said.

"OK. Let's hope for better news in the morning then," Lyons said.

* * *

When the room had cleared, Hays and Lyons went off to her office.

"I'm very uneasy about Williams," she said.

"Me too. What happened with his car?"

"It's still out there somewhere, I guess. We didn't move it anyway. Why?" she said.

"Two things. Firstly, if he's used to having his wicked way with the fifth and sixth form girls, then I suspect the back seat of his car might provide some interesting samples for Sinéad to analyse. And secondly, if we had his car, then he couldn't use it, could he?"

"Very true. Why don't we go back out to the school and find out from him exactly where it is and get the keys? Then we can drive out and collect it. It's better than sitting here doing nothing waiting for the forensics," Lyons said.

"Good idea. I'm sure Mr O'Connell will be delighted to see us so soon again. Oh, and we'd better put Pascal in the picture too. It's his patch, after all."

* * *

"Ah, hello again, Mr O'Connell. We just need a word with Mr Williams. Is he in?" Lyons said as they met the headmaster coming out of his house.

"I don't think so, I haven't seen him. I thought he was helping you with your enquiries."

"He's out on bail for the moment," Hays said.

"Well I don't think he's here, but go on up to his flat if you like. The door is open," O'Connell said, and he walked off across towards one of the classrooms.

Williams wasn't in his flat, and there was no sign that he'd been there at all.

"That's a bit odd. Where else would he go?" Lyons said.

"Search me. Anyway, I'll give Pascal a call and see if he has any idea where Williams' car is, and then maybe we can go and get it. At least then the whole day won't have been a complete waste of time," Hays said.

Hays dialled the number for Roundstone.

"Ah, hello Pascal, it's Superintendent Hays here." As he spoke into the phone, he could almost see the young Garda sitting up straight on hearing who it was. "We were wondering if Williams' car had showed up anywhere around?"

"Oh yes, right. It has, as it happens. One of the patrols saw it parked over near the harbour at Carna. It's a blue Ford Focus 09 G something or other. It's registered to him," Brosnan said.

"OK, Pascal, good work. Inspector Lyons and I are going to come out and collect it. We need to bring it back in for forensics to have a look at. So, if anyone reports someone breaking into it and taking it away, don't panic, it will be one of us," Hays said.

"Oh, right so. I'll let the lads know. Will you be calling in?" Brosnan asked.

"No, not this time, Pascal. Your stash of chocolate biscuits is safe! Thanks, bye."

"How are we going to get into his car and get it started without the keys, Maureen?" Hays said when he had finished the call.

"Fear not, Superintendent. But you may have to hide your eyes for a minute or two!" Lyons said.

* * *

It was a fine summer evening as Hays and Lyons drove out towards Carna. The scenery was stunning, and as the sun began to set gently in the western sky, the long shadows cast by the mountains created a pretty pattern on the bogland. The water in the many lakes that they passed looked like silver as the low sun reflected on the still surfaces.

They found Williams' Ford Focus where Pascal Brosnan had said it would be. It was in pretty good condition for a car almost ten years old. Lyons got out of Hays' Mercedes and walked over to it. She waved back to Hays, gesturing for him to turn away, as she took the little black plastic device out of her jacket pocket, and pressed the larger of two buttons. The red light flashed for a few seconds, and then as it went green, the door locks on the Focus popped, and she was able to open the door.

She walked back over to where Hays was parked with the driver's window wound down.

"Not just a pretty face, are you?" he smiled.

"Isn't eBay wonderful? And for my next trick, ladies and gentlemen," she said, taking an exaggerated bow, "I'll start the old banger and drive away. Bye now!" And she did just exactly that.

On the way back to town, Hays called Sinéad Loughran on the hands-free phone and advised her that they were bringing in Williams' car. He asked her to get someone working on it as soon as possible, and to concentrate on the back seat and floor area to see if any traces of either Emma Fortune or Amy Cunningham could be found in it.

When Lyons had left the car in the secure yard at the back of Mill Street Garda station, she got back into Hays' Mercedes.

"Where did you get that natty little gizmo?" he said.

"On eBay. It only cost thirty quid. Came from eastern Europe. I didn't think it would work, but there you go."

"I presume it's highly illegal to even have one of those in your possession," Hays said.

"Oohh, are you going to arrest me and put me in handcuffs, Superintendent?" she said, laughing.

Chapter Twenty-seven

The following morning, Maureen received a call from forensic services.

"Hi, Maureen, it's Sinéad. Listen, we have some results back on various things now. Is it OK if I pop over in a few minutes?" Loughran said.

"Great, yes, sure. See you soon."

Lyons got the team together in the briefing room. They were all there except for Hays, who was off on some official duty somewhere.

Sinéad Loughran came in, and wasted no time in getting started.

"OK. Well, we have a few different sets of results. Firstly, we found hair samples from both Amy Cunningham and Emma Fortune on the duvet in the forepeak of Williams' boat. And some other hair samples from other girls, as yet unidentified. We also found several semen stains and other bodily fluid residue on the bed, and that's away for analysis as we speak. It seems Mr Williams wasn't too careful about laundering his bedlinen."

A murmur went around the room.

"And now for the good news," Loughran went on, "the plastic tube. The piece taken from the plane matches exactly the tubing we recovered from Williams' flat. It's not that it's just the same type – the cut at the end of the pipe that was connected to the carburettor shows that it was taken from the same length of piping that we found at the flat. And it gets better. There was a small smudge of blood caught in the ragged cut end. It looks like the tubing was cut with a rather blunt knife, maybe a Stanley knife or something, and we found such an implement in the boot of Williams' car. I'm having it tested as we speak."

Eamon Flynn spoke up. "Oh, wow, that figures. I remember when I was taking Williams' fingerprints, he had a small nick on the pad of his thumb. Just like you'd get if you were rolling a plastic thing against the blade of a knife, and it cut through."

"Nice one. Let's hope the blood sample on the pipe is a match for Williams. That would be very hard for him to explain," Lyons said.

John O'Connor, who had been listening intensely to Loughran's revelations, put his hand up.

"Yes, John. What have you got?" Lyons asked.

"Well, I finally managed to get into Williams' chatroom activity. I was able to match messages with a timeline where he and Emma were chatting. Some of it was pretty salacious. But, perhaps more importantly, just recently, Emma must have found out something about him that she didn't like. She started calling him all the names, and said she was going to tell her parents and the school what he had been up to. She was pretty het up," O'Connor said.

"That's great work, folks. We have enough now to hold him for the murders. John, keep digging on his computer. See if you can find any searches where he was looking up aircraft engines or anything like that. We're going to nail this bastard, and soon. Trouble is, we have to find him first! Sally, will you alert everyone that Williams is wanted for questioning in connection with a triple murder? Eamon, can you take Mary out to the school, and see if there's been any sign? James, you come with me. We need to try and figure where this dude is hiding out," Lyons said.

Back in her office, Lyons and Bolger were getting their heads together when the phone rang.

"Inspector Lyons? This is Pascal Brosnan out in Roundstone. Listen, I've got some bad news, I'm afraid."

"Hi Pascal. Go on."

"You know that boat that we had tied up down at the harbour here? Well, it's gone."

"Gone! What do you mean, gone? Where has it gone?" Lyons said.

"I don't know, Inspector. I was down there early this morning getting the paper, and I went down to check on it, and there it was, all gone," Brosnan said.

"Jesus, Pascal. It must be Williams. He's disappeared too. He must have taken off in it. He could be anywhere. Look, can you stay in the station there till I get back to you?" Lyons said. Bolger was signalling furiously with his hands to attract Lyons' attention, so she told Brosnan to hold on, and put her hand over the telephone receiver.

"Ask him if he knows anyone with a fast boat out there, maybe a RIB or something," Bolger said.

Lyons relayed the message.

"There is a fella out the road a bit that has one, I think. He uses it to take tourists out to some of the islands close to the village here. I'll give him a call and see if he can bring it down to the harbour. Will you come out?"

"Yes, we're on our way."

Lyons and Bolger grabbed radios and some waterproof jackets and ran to the car park. Lyons took one of the marked cars, and left Mill Street with the sirens screaming and blue lights flashing as she drove quickly towards the N59.

When they were underway, Lyons said to Bolger, "James, get onto air sea rescue at Shannon. See if they would be prepared to get their helicopter up to scour the area out west of Roundstone. I don't know where this guy is headed, but we need to find him. There's a radio in my jacket that you can use once they are airborne."

It took them just over an hour to get to the harbour in Roundstone. Brosnan was there, and the man with the bright orange RIB was there too, with the boat already launched and bobbing about in the water.

Brosnan introduced Darragh Egan as the owner of the powerful looking vessel.

"Don't worry, Inspector. He only has nine horse power, we'll have seventy. If he's out there, we'll catch him."

As they boarded the inflatable, they heard the heavy throb of the coastguard helicopter overhead.

Lyons spoke to the pilot and explained what they were doing, and agreed that the helicopter would search the sea space and report back to the RIB if they found anything. It wasn't long before they heard from the chopper.

"There's a yacht under sail heading north, some six nautical miles from your position." The pilot went on to give the co-ordinates of the boat.

"I have GPS on board. I can steer to that location. We'll be there in twenty minutes," Egan said.

It wasn't long before they could see the shape of the thirty-foot sloop with its large white sails, gently heeled over, using the south westerly breeze to ply along at a brisk pace.

"Any chance we could try and sneak up on him, approach from the lee side where his sails might obstruct his view of us," Lyons shouted to Egan.

"I can try, but he'll probably hear my engine if he's just on sail power," Egan said.

They ploughed on through the gentle aquamarine swell until they could see Derek Williams clearly on board, sitting down low in the cockpit of his yacht.

He saw them too, and must have realised what was happening. He disappeared below decks for a couple of minutes, and then reappeared.

As the RIB got close, Egan said to Lyons, "There's something wrong. She's lying too low in the water. Look, the sea is slopping over the side. I think she's sinking!"

On board the yacht, Williams had gone below and opened the sea cocks. Seawater was rushing into the boat at a fast pace, and the main cabin was already calf deep in it. Williams reached to the stern of the boat, and pulled the small Avon dinghy that was being towed along behind the yacht by its painter, till it was up against the pushpit. He then climbed over the rear guardrail and dropped into the dinghy, untying the painter from the mothership and drifting away. By the time Egan had caught up to him,

Williams' yacht was awash, and close to going under. There was nothing anyone could do – the boat was heading for the bottom, and any further evidence that it contained was going with it.

Egan, who turned out to be a very skilled helmsman, brought the larger orange RIB alongside the smaller Avon dinghy.

"We need you to come aboard, Mr Williams," Lyons said as the two boats chafed against each other uncomfortably.

"You want me, come and get me," Williams replied defiantly.

"Right, James, over you go," Lyons said.

Bolger gave her a dirty look, but did as he was told. A couple of seconds later, he was in the Avon with Williams, and had the suspect handcuffed, with his hands behind his back. Bolger then passed the long rope attached to the bow of the dinghy to Egan who made it fast, and they began to tow it back towards Roundstone.

As they motored away from the scene, Williams' yacht gave a few bubbly gasps and went down by the head, never to be seen again.

Chapter Twenty-eight

"And what have you charged my client with this time, Inspector, littering the pavement?" Ernest Joyce said when he entered the station at Mill Street and got talking to Lyons.

"How does three counts of murder, one of attempted murder and arson grab you, Mr Joyce, plus a whole host of other offences to do with aviation? The list is so long, I can't remember it all," Lyons said.

"And I presume you have…"

"Yes, Mr Joyce, we have lots and lots and lots of excellent evidence, so can we stop wasting our time and get on with it?" Lyons interrupted.

In the interview room Williams was bombarded with all the evidence that the team had gathered.

There were the hair samples that had been found on his boat, and the other bio material that Sinéad Loughran had recovered before Williams had scuppered the yacht.

There was the plastic pipe, complete with a trace of Williams blood on it, and a cut across it that exactly matched the corresponding pattern on the tubing found in Williams' home wine making kit.

There was the Stanley knife found in the boot of Williams' car.

There was the chatroom interaction between Emma Fortune and Williams, where Emma had threatened to expose him for having sex with his pupils – some of whom were underage, making it statutory rape.

John O'Connor had found that before the plane crash, Williams had been searching for details of the fuel system on Lycoming engines, as fitted to almost every Cessna 172 that was ever made.

There was the thumb print on the lock that had been found in the grass out at the hangar at Galway airport.

Print outs and screen shots of the incriminating messages and Williams' search activities were produced.

Throughout the interview, Williams, and surprisingly, his solicitor, remained almost completely silent. When Lyons had exhausted all the evidence, she looked Williams dead in the eye, and said, "You must have something to say, Mr Williams. Your silence could be interpreted by a jury as an admission of guilt, or at least as contemptuous. It isn't going to do you any good in the long run."

Joyce responded on his client's behalf.

"I wonder if I could have a few minutes to confer with my client, Inspector."

"Certainly. I need a break anyway. Shall we say fifteen minutes?"

"Thank you, yes, that would be fine."

* * *

When Lyons and Bolger re-entered the interview room, Williams was sitting with his arms folded in front of him, looking sullen. Joyce, however, was in a much cheerier mood.

"My client is prepared to admit to a number of, shall we say, mistakes that he has made in an effort to preserve his reputation from hysterical schoolgirls, and let's be honest, much of the evidence you have shown us here today is very circumstantial. We could probably accept manslaughter on one count, and then maybe the other matters could be left where they are?" Joyce said rather hopefully.

Lyons looked the solicitor straight in the eye.

"I think we'll let the jury decide on the veracity of our evidence, shall we? James, would you be so kind as to charge Mr Williams here with three counts of murder; rape; arson; attempted murder; offences under the Wireless and Telegraphy act 1926, as amended, and anything else that our evidence has revealed, and see if you can get him remanded before Judge Meehan. That will be all, Mr Joyce." She turned and left the room.

"Christ, how much raw meat did she have for breakfast?" Joyce said to Bolger when Lyons had left the room.

"I think it was his attempt to burn her alive out at the hangar that did it. Oh, and she doesn't like boats either!" Bolger said.

* * *

"Come in, James, take a seat, would you like a coffee?" Hays said as James Bolger entered his rather plush office on the top floor of the Mill Street Garda station. "I just wanted to have a word with you about how you're finding things here – a sort of unofficial review, if you will."

"Thanks, sir. Not too good to be honest. I'm not sure that I'm cut out for this type of work. It all looked so easy on paper when I was studying criminology, but it's very different in reality, isn't it?" Bolger said.

"Yes, it is indeed. Look, I'm not going to try and persuade you to give it more of a chance or anything like that. You're an adult, and you know your own mind best. But I would like to know what your intentions are, if you know them at this stage."

"I think I'd like to move on, sir. It doesn't have to be immediate if it would make things awkward for you with Chief Superintendent Plunkett. But maybe a transfer to some other area of the force that isn't so, well, in your face, if you'll pardon the expression."

"Yes, I know what you mean. Leave it with me for a few days. I'm sure we can use your obvious talents elsewhere to good effect. I wouldn't want to lose you altogether, so I'll have a snoop around, see if we can come up with something that suits everyone. Are you keen to stay in this region?" Hays said.

"Well, I hope this doesn't cause offence, but no actually. I'd rather be back in Dublin, if that's possible."

"Understood. As I say, leave it with me. I have some good connections in HQ. I'm sure we'll be able to sort something out."

* * *

When Lyons got back to the squad room, a spontaneous round of applause greeted her. Shouts of "well done" and "congratulations, boss" rang out across the room. The entire team was there: Eamon Flynn, Sally Fahy, Mary Costelloe, Liam Walsh, John O'Connor, and Sinéad Loughran, who had come across from her laboratory. When the noise settled down, it was clear the assembled crowd were expecting some form of response from Lyons.

"OK, OK, thanks everybody. I only have one thing to say," she said with a serious face, "I don't ever want to have to arrest a suspect in a fucking rubber dinghy again, EVER!"

The whole team, including herself, laughed out loud.

Character List

Superintendent Mick Hays – newly promoted to Superintendent, Hays longs for some "real" police work.

Senior Inspector Maureen Lyons – the feisty Garda who is also Hays' partner.

Inspector James Bolger – a new recruit in the force's attempt to modernize.

Detective Sergeant Eamon Flynn – an observant and tenacious Garda who never lets go.

Detective Sergeant Sally Fahy – an ex-civilian worker who loves police work.

Detective Garda Mary Costelloe – a new member of the team who shows great promise.

Detective Garda Liam Walsh – recently promoted from the uniformed ranks. Will he make the grade?

Garda John O'Connor – the unit's tech-savvy assistant.

Sinéad Loughran – the forensic team leader with a good nose for wrongdoing.

Garda Pascal Brosnan – the lone Garda in charge of Roundstone Garda station.

Garda Jim Dolan – based in Clifden, Dolan doesn't like too much work-related stress.

Garda Peadar Tobin – a good-looking young Garda with chivalrous tendencies.

Sergeant Séan Mulholland – a wily old Garda who runs the station in Clifden in his own unique way.

Fergal O'Dwyer – an accident investigator from the Irish Aviation Authority.

Sandra Jameson – O'Dwyer's assistant.

Brian O'Neill – a highly skilled helicopter pilot who works for the coastguard.

Jane Wells – O'Neill's equally highly skilled co-pilot.

Ger Fortune – the well-to-do builder who made good during the Celtic Tiger.

Barbara Fortune – Ger Fortune's wife.

Fionn Devaney – an architect with big ideas.

Mrs Devaney – Fionn's wife.

Emma Fortune – Ger Fortune's pretty seventeen-year-old daughter.

Amy Cunningham – Emma Fortune's best friend.

Donal O'Connell – headmaster at Emma and Amy's school.

Derek Williams – Emma's form teacher and games master.

Charlie Willis – runs the flying club based at Galway airport.

Terry Normoyle – a highly experienced aircraft engineer.

Séan McCreedy – station manager at the airport on Inis Mór.

Paddy Lavelle – owns a fishing boat that he keeps in Roundstone harbour.

Darragh Egan – has a fast rigid-hulled inflatable boat that he uses for tourist trips in and around Bertraghboy Bay.

Ernest Joyce – a Galway solicitor.

James McMahon – an architect from Galway who is well known to the Gardaí.

Tony Fallon – used to have his own business, but now works in forestry.